Scripts from the Underworld

Selected Works

Jean-Paul Corriveau

To KB
my Scottish brother!
JP

ISBN: 1-4636-5782-X
ISBN-13: 9781463657826

Contents

A Light in Avalon

Luce jerked his body off the bed a few inches as the alarm cried out and signaled his ten a.m. wake up time. He turned his body to hit the alarm, but of course there was nothing to strike since the alarm was emitted from numerous tiny speakers planted in each of the surrounding walls.

His action shocked him. He had tried to turn off the alarm with his own hand. Why? Luce shook his head and removed the last vestiges of sleep from his mind, trying to figure out what had just happened, and he drew in a deep breath to speak.

"Off," he yelled. Immediately, the annoying sound of the alarm ceased to blare.

Luce lay in bed thinking about what he had just attempted to do. It was amazing. He had actually tried to act on his own. What did it mean? People didn't need to do anything for themselves; that was what the machines were for and why the voice commands were set up.

Above him, the metal tentacles writhed in anticipation of his command to be picked up out of bed. They shifted about in snakelike fashion, and the whirring of the engines running them almost sounded like demons hissing. Not that Luce knew what snakes or demons were or what properties they bore. No human had seen animals for nearly a hundred years, and the last that had did not pass on that information about other life forms to their descendents. As far as Luce was concerned, humans and their metal machines were the only existing objects in his boxlike world.

Luce turned his head and stared at his airchair. The egg-shaped conveyance hovered silently about a foot above the ground, and the red light registering an inactive status blinked repeatedly. Off. On. Off. It seemed to Luce that the machine was trying to convey some important message to him in its strange electronic language. What was it say? Luce watched the light for a few more minutes, but no answer came to him. No clue provided insight into the chair's mysterious language, so Luce turned his head upwards again and let his eyes de-focus upon the servant tentacles while he tried to think.

Why had he attempted to manually turn off the alarm? He had never done that before now. Hell, no one had done that previously that he knew. Or had someone? He would have to ask Mol. Mol did some odd things, like grab for people's ears as he whisked past them in his airchair. It was a bizarre thing to try to use one's arms and hands. It made his chest feel funny. But he had done it instinctively, hadn't he? He didn't consciously decide to reach for the alarm; he had just done it. Did that mean that it was natural to use one's arms? If so, why was it that people didn't? Why then did they have all these machines to do things for them?

"Up," he commanded, and the tentacles rapidly descended from the ceiling to remove the covers from his body. Two of the tentacles shot to the far side of the room to deposit the sheets in the cloth disposal unit, while the other four gently wrapped around Luce's corpulent body and lifted him off the bed. He remained completely relaxed as they transported him to the washing unit.

The wash unit was a large plastic basin located to the side of the kitchenette. Three large hoses hung down from the ceiling over the basin: one sprayed water at a fairly high velocity, one exuded thick, sweet-smelling soap suds, and the last ejected a blast of warm air. Each of them moved independent of the others and coiled about like the tentacles holding Luce. Luce remained limp and let the hoses spray his large pale body with suds and water. Suddenly, an odd impulse entered his head, and he began smearing the soap suds around his body in an effort to clean himself better. His arms moved awkwardly, unused to the strain of physical activity, but the sensation he received from their motions relaxed him in a way that he had not felt prior to now. He liked this strange feeling. He wanted it to continue, but he was not sure whether it resulted from the simple movement of his appendages or from their frictional contact upon his flesh. He decided to try an experiment to find out.

When the air hose had finished drying him off, Luce ordered the tentacles to set him down. They began to carry him to his airchair across the room, but he yelled out, "down, now!" so that they hesitantly dropped him onto the cold surface of the floor. Luce lay still for a few moments while the tentacles moved about in confusion above him.

It was not easy to sit up on one's own power. Usually, the airchair provided some form of stability for the body to rest against, but without the chair it required a weird sense of balance and bodily strength. Luce fell over onto his side twice before finally adjusting his equilibrium properly.

Luce sat there and listened to his heart pound. His heart never beat that rapidly except when the machines brought him to orgasm in the Stim Room. This pulse, as opposed to his sexual one, was more irregular. It frightened him, and he wasn't sure that he liked this aspect of self control. He pushed these thoughts aside, though. If he was going to learn the mystery behind acting on one's own, he was going to have to accept the bad with the good. There was no middle ground.

A buzzing sound alerted him to the appearance of an incoming holo-message. Lasers shot forth from each of the room's walls, striking together two feet in front of Luce, and presently a three dimensional likeness of Mol appeared before his eyes. The crackling figurine reclined glassy-eyed and addressed Luce in short clipped speech.

"Hey…Luce. It's Mol. I'm going to the Chem Room. Meet me there, and we'll colorize. I have a surprise."

The image disappeared.

Luce stared for a few seconds at the space where Mol had just appeared, then felt the cold touch of the floor against his bare flesh and realized that he needed to get dressed. Luce turned to look at his hanging robes that were situated near the bed. He began to crawl slowly toward them as the tentacles continued to hover nervously nearby, anticipating any sudden command.

Today, he would dress himself, he decided. No matter how difficult it would be, he would dress himself.

Luce was almost walking. His upper torso lay flat upon the back of the airchair while his legs held a limited amount of his weight and plodded forward heavily, and what felt like extreme heat extended up both calves. His face shone with sweat. It burned red like a devil's face, and people passing in their airchairs glanced at him in fright before commanding their chairs to increase their speed away from him. Luce didn't see what was so terrifying about his actions. He could not understand the fear in their eyes.

The corridor turned right, and at the end Luce could see the entranceway to the Chem Room. The time it had taken him to walk here had seemed interminably long. He had spent most of the time staring up at the light tracks that ran along the ceiling and telling himself over and over, "I can do it. I can do it." After minutes of repetition, he could almost believe that the painful heat in his legs had disappeared and that he was floating lightly upon celestial clouds of smoke. He even felt for a moment that he was able to fully support himself and walk without the assistance of the airchair. The strangeness of this imagined sensation seemed pleasant.

The Chem Room was the most popular room to utilize. Its dimly lit confines offered a dreamy haven for Luce's peers, with its opiate based drugs and bubbles of merging color on the ceiling. The majority of the populace lounged here inhaling the hallucinogenic smoke and gazed upwards in the hopes of finding transcendental visions in the moving patterns of color displayed by the lasers.

There were even more people here today than usual. The aisles left barely enough space for the airchair to pass through, and Luce in his exhaustion had a difficult time moving along the rows in search of Mol. A good portion of those present were very old men. Women, unlike the men, often found more satisfying pleasure in floating through the children's wards where they would teach the mid-range ones to speak or would hum faint snatches of melody to the youngest. The women that came to the Chem Room tended to be at that indistinct age between youth and adulthood.

Luce glanced at all the old men lying inert in their airchairs. Drool ran down their chins. Their breathing seemed forced, and Luce found himself trying to recall whether he had ever seen any older women lying around covered in their own body fluids. He could not. The only females Luce could conjure up in his mind were young, childlike ones or those that were immediately in adulthood. It was as if the older women did not exist. Yet how could they not? If old men could be found lying around or speeding down corridors, then old women had to be here also. It was only logical, but the question arose, "where were they?"

"Hey, Luce! Over here."

Mol's voice drew Luce out of his reverie. Mol had positioned his airchair in the corner of the room, as he usually did, and he was waving his hand to catch Luce's attention. Normally, Mol's motioning attracted the disapproving gaze of their fellow Chem Roomers, but today it was Luce's irregular attempt to walk that held their eyes. They stared at him in outright scorn.

Luce hardly noticed. He found himself drawn to the side of Mol's airchair where a wild design had been painted.

"Like it?" Mol queried. "I thought it up myself. I was in the Wash Unit this morning getting bathed when I seemed to float up out of my body and examine myself. I don't know why, but for some reason I thought it might be neat to have my vision colored onto the side of my airchair. I asked the tentacles to assist me."

Mol smiled that distinctive, childlike grin of his, while Luce appraised his handiwork. He continued to talk. "It took me forever to find something to use to mark it with, but eventually, I realized that the berry pie we get from the food dispenser would make a great colorizer so I ordered two plates of it."

Luce half stood there, studying the tentacle's handiwork. It appeared that the berry juice depicted an upright-postured man who held his arms straight out at his sides and seemed to hang upon the air. The positioning of the body formed bisecting lines that were perpendicular to each other and effectively transfixed the viewer. Luce could not pry his eyes off of it. There was some meaning there that could not easily be deciphered. He could not shake the feeling that whatever enigma it contained was important...to him and all his peers.

The following weeks plodded slowly by. Each day, Luce spent his time walking up and down the corridors with the assistance of his airchair, and each day his strength increased. People floated past him in confusion, anger, or fear. They could not understand his rationale for acting in such a grotesque fashion. One young girl even attempted to strike him down with her chair. She had spied him from some distance down the straightaway that turned onto the Stim Room corridor, and she had commanded her chair to aim for him at full speed. At the last moment, Luce had let himself fall to the floor, and she had careened off the side of his chair directly above his head before she sped off into the distance.

Mol, in turn, had been intrigued but not too supportive of Luce's new activity. He could not see the point of it all when one could simply lie back and relax in the Chem Room and let the time drift by in leisure.

"Moving one's hands is one thing, Luce, but this leg action. It's sick. Why are you doing it? I know it doesn't feel good; I can see it on your face. Maybe you have one of those rare mind problems. Maybe you should head to the Med Room and get looked at by the compudoc, because you are acting a bit weird."

Luce stifled his disappointment with Mol, ignored everybody else's comments, and continued to build up his strength and muscle tone despite them all. He even stopped going to the Chem Room on a regular basis, and on the days that he didn't attend he noticed that his walking ability improved, an observation which caused him to make fewer and fewer trips there. He started feeling healthy and exhilarated, learning to walk, and he decided to stop caring whether others thought he was acting inappropriately or improperly. He knew deep inside that he was not.

Early one morning, Luce decided to walk a new corridor and headed in the direction of the Children's Wards. The passage appeared brighter than the one's near the Chem Room and Stim Room. Pastel colors adorned the side walls, and it actually felt uplifting compared to the other gloomy passageways. Luce gazed at the change in his surroundings and smiled.

About two-thirds of the way along the entrance corridor, Luce noticed a dark segment of the wall that contrasted with the brightly painted nature of the rest of the hall. He stopped his shuffling progress to study it and realized that it was not actually a shadowed part of the wall but instead the aperture to a separate corridor.

Why hadn't he seen it before?

Luce guided his airchair over to the opening and peered inside. No lights illuminated the hallway, and he had no way of determining how far back it went. Luce commanded his airchair to move into the passage, but it refused to motorize in that direction. As he continued to yell at his unresponsive conveyance he realized that it was too large to squeeze into the dark hall's narrow confines. Suddenly, he understood why the passage was dark and its presence unknown until now. This hallway had been sitting unused for lifetimes because everyone speeding by would not be able to notice the shadowy patch in the wall. Even if his peers were able to see the lighting change in this spot, it would probably give them little cause to wonder, being little more than a blur as they passed by. Nothing was drastically unusual. Only by learning to walk and moving slowly was he able to observe its existence.

Luce couldn't overlook this call to adventure. Now that he was walking, he had to follow the path to its destination and uncover the mysteries at the end of the passage.

"It is now or never," he thought. Luce pushed his upper torso off the edge of the airchair. Both arms shook violently, and he expected his body to plunge back to its original position. Fortunately, that did not occur. To his surprise, he remained completely upright. His head felt airy. A cool breeze glided through his mind, and it carried the heaviness of the past years with it. He laughed giddily.

The sudden elation would not last. With the very first step he placed, fear came sweeping in. His body tilted rapidly from left to right, threatening to slam him to the ground, and his arms flailed about chaotically. He was immediately forced to exert all his energy to maintain a vertical stance. Somehow, he managed to do so, but he had to pause for a few moments to regain his equilibrium.

On his second step, he almost overcompensated when he tried to avoid tilting too far forward. He realized his mistake just in time. By his third step, his fear had mostly left him, and he took a number of short, rapid steps to cover a greater distance. He was deep in the darkened corridor, now, and had to lean against the cold metal wall for support and rest. Behind him, the gears of the airchair whirred nervously. Luce turned his head to gaze back the way he had come, and he realized that he couldn't proceed further into the passage without risking injury. This was a perfect situation for utilizing the airchair's front light. Luce threw his voice back down the hall and commanded the chair to illuminate his way. It abruptly turned to face him, and it shot a beam of yellow light down the corridor from its frontal fixture, blinding Luce temporarily with its brilliance.

The hallway wasn't as long as Luce had expected. It extended five feet past the point at which Luce had stopped and ended at a strange looking door with two amber stripes running down its center on either side of the separation crack. Luce staggered up to it slowly. He placed his hand against its smooth surface and felt the vibration of energy.

"The door still functions, at least," he thought, connecting its vibratory nature with the similar one that he felt in his airchair each day.

"Open," he directed, and the door slid with a vaporous hiss in two separate directions into the wall. The newly created aperture opened onto a small, gray cubicle with no noticeable egresses, and Luce wondered what possible function it could serve being simply a tiny barren room. Luce staggered inside, anyway, grunting as his considerable bulk made his passage through the doorway difficult. To his shock, the door slid shut behind him. He was unsure of what to do, finding himself trapped.

"Level?" rang out a gravelly metallic voice. Luce was bewildered; he had never heard a machine speak before. The machines only communicated through flashes of light or some coded electronic manner. Was this machine alive?

"What do you mean by level?" he queried in response.

"What is your floor designation?"

Luce pondered the meaning of the exotic terms. Floor? Level? He had never heard these words used by anyone he had spoken with, not even Mol. And Designation? His mouth stumbled over the syllables trying to pronounce the lengthy word.

"Floor number, please," the machine reiterated.

Number. That was a term that Luce could understand. It dealt with how many pies one asked the machine for or how many people were visiting his room at one time. He felt confident enough to answer now.

"Two."

A whining sound erupted from each of the walls. Luce felt unnaturally heavy. His weak legs could not stand the strain of the abrupt ascent of the cubicle, and he sank to the floor, his face a mask of bewilderment. His arms lashed out instinctively for a handhold.

Abruptly, the heaviness departed. Luce raised his head and watched as the door slid open again to reveal a dimly lit hallway. His airchair and the hidden corridor were nowhere in sight. Confusion suffused him as he struggled to his feet. Where was he?

Luce stood transfixed on the view before him. He had moved down the hall, turned right, and arrived at a door on his left. The passageway continued on for a distance before T-ing off in two directions, but Luce had decided to check behind the door. It opened onto a room that reminded him of the Med Room. It had the same set up and machines that the Med Room had, except something felt very wrong. Luce couldn't quite place the reason for the disturbance from the doorway.

Taking a step forward, Luce spied the numerous spec-op tentacles hanging limply down from each wall. Some had scalpels on their tips, some had suction tubes, some had suture clamps, and others had even more unique and indefinable appendages. For the most part, they appeared to be normal.

The Compudoc sat in its normal place on the ceiling, but all of its lights were dark and its probes rigidly still. It hovered menacingly over the examination table placed squarely in the center of the room, and it engulfed the table like the sometimes ominous smoky bursts of gases that billowed over the heads of him and his friends in the Chem Room. Something looked unusual about the examination table. It had been crafted out of pure metal, and one end of the table had two silver rods rise up a foot above each corner to end in strange thick-ringed attachments. Two more metal rings, similar to the ones atop the rods, were positioned further up the table on either side, and Luce could not comprehend what purpose they served.

Across the room, a crimson glow caught Luce's attention. He glanced up to see that it emanated from a side chamber opposite the door he had entered, and some deep corner of his brain told him that it would prove to be the source of his odd nervousness. Luce decided to cross the room to investigate.

As he stepped into the expansive second room, he found himself greeted by a horrific sight. Female bodies lay stacked to the ceiling, many decayed, and the stench forced Luce to vomit uncontrollably. All about him, the piles of flesh stretched back into the far reaches of this cavernous chamber and formed a seemingly endless range of corpse-created mountains where arms entangled other arms and legs jutted out at various angles. The sight made him gag. Breathless lips kissed gangrenous nipples, while stringy tangles of hair covered blackened eye sockets or protrusions of bone. Once ivory skin bore blotchy stains of dried blood, and once active tongues dangled fetidly in gaping mouths. Luce almost tumbled to floor nauseated.

Luce could not comprehend what death was. All he understood was that these bodies no longer moved and that their eyes had gone sightless. The scene both awed and disgusted him. His mind swirled with half-formed thoughts and ideas, the foremost being that life was not always life. He had heard rumors about people disappearing, but he had not heeded them. He had thought that they were just that, rumors. Obviously, they weren't, and this must be the place where they ended up, though he had to wonder where the men's bodies were.

"Perhaps in another room," he reasoned, yet this made little sense to him.

Luce didn't have time to consider the horror further. A slightly human sounding voice greeted him from behind.

"Well, well, well. A human male on the upper levels. It has been quite some time since I have seen one of you in a functional mode. This is an honor."

Luce turned swiftly to find himself face to face with a metal person. But how could this be? What sort of magic could create a nearly human machine? Involuntarily, Luce started to step away from the thing, but something soft and squishy under his foot stopped him. He glanced down to see the bloody remains of what looked like a male child with some sort of fleshy tentacle erupting from its stomach. Quickly, he looked away. The urge to vomit rose up in him again.

"Do not worry," the gray metal being soothed, "I am not going to hurt you. I work for you."

"What are you?" Luce asked fearfully. "You look like a man, but you're a machine."

"My name is Gabe, my good man. Code number I 14 7 5 12—777 division of the Avalon series. I am what your kind would call a robot, a synthetic human. I oversee the upper decks."

"You oversee the what?"

"The upper decks, of this ship...the Avalon. I was created specifically for duty here."

"What is a ship?"

The robot faked a human sigh and proceeded to study Luce's body. "I suppose it has been a long time, hasn't it? You have all forgotten you past. Of course, it should be expected. You cannot obtain total bliss without paying some price."

Luce stared at the robot in confusion. Bliss? The thing spoke a number of strange words, and he was having trouble following its line of conversation. What was going on? He wanted to understand what it was saying to him, but he was too frightened and confused at the moment to question it further. He remained silent and watched it closely as it examined him.

"I have an idea," the robot continued. "You should accompany me. I will explain everything. If I say so, myself, it is fortunate that one of you finally decided to travel up here because the situation has been deteriorating of late. The Agrideck has become overgrown with weeds, many of the crops rot, and the water tanks have started to rust and poison the water. Mich, Raph, Zaph, and I have been working to stave off the inevitable, but we are only a few. Too many of the other 777's have broken down, and our attempts at performing the duties others had on top of our own are not sufficient. What is worse is that the central computer has misinterpreted, or deliberately altered, Captain Al's last directive. We have wanted to try and rectify the problem ourselves, but we are robots and therefore have no authority in commanding the computer to reconfigure itself. You, though, can."

Luce glanced around the room again. His head spun with the words issued by the robot and with the horrifying nature of the room about him. The two stimuli stirred up a whirlwind in his mind, disrupting his equilibrium, and he barely noticed that the robot ushered him back out toward the corridor. As the two crossed back through the alternative Med Room, Luce distantly observed an angry, naked woman being hauled into the room by a couple of boxlike machines. The Med Room tentacles promptly sprang forth from the wall to seize her and immobilize her upon the examination table. She continued to struggles as they placed her arms and legs inside of the metal rings. Apparently, they were restraining devices. Luce wanted to help free the woman, but his mind seemed completely divorced from his body due to the overwhelming nature of all his recent revelations. He felt that he could not act in any manner whatsoever, and he simply gazed in awe at how large and round the woman's belly appeared. As he was escorted closer to the door, a tentacle ending in a scalpel whipped across the room and deftly sliced open the woman's stomach like a piece of fruit. The sight jolted Luce back to lucidity, but by that time the robot had completely pushed him into the hallway and commanded the door to close. The robot seated him on a hovering platform, stared at him for a few moments to gauge his status, and seemed to contemplate something inscrutable. After a short passing of time, it commanded the hovering platform to head toward the 'elevator'. It led the way with the platform following, and Luce sat there befuddled. He could not determine if he was here in this strange hallway or back in the Chem Room inhaling the mind dulling smoke. In either case, he was no longer enjoying the sensation.

The robot led him into a cubicle much like the one he had exited previously and informed him that he would be transporting Luce to the Bridge where Captain Al could be found. Luce started to feel less light headed. His mind had apparently found some way to connect with his body again, and having temporarily suppressed the awful visions he had just witnessed, he found that he wanted to meet this person, Al.

"Al must be an interesting person," Luce told himself, "if he can live alone in these strange corridors with only metal men for company. Patiently, he waited for the door to slide open. He was prepared to see a completely new set of corridors, just as he had experienced on Level Two. What he actually saw ended up being much more amazing.

The Bridge turned out to be an enormous room with the ceiling rising to the great height of twenty-five feet above the floor. The floor itself dropped downward two steps to form a mini arena, and it created the perception that the room existed inside some gigantic sphere. Large black screens showing an array of white dots covered one whole concave wall, and the center of the room contained what looked like embryonic airchairs that had been connected to the floor with metal struts and placed in front of odd, geometrically square companion units. The vast grandeur of the place astonished Luce.

"Impressive, is it not?" Gabe spoke for him. "This is where the magic happens, the Command Module, though no one has occupied it for many years."

Finally, the robot had mentioned something that Luce could grasp. Eagerly, he questioned it again to gain understanding of the reason for this place.

"What do you mean, command? Command what?"

"Why, the ship, of course. You guide it from this location."

Luce grew irritated. "There you go mentioning a ship again. What is this thing, this ship?"

"It is this spacecraft. It is what we presently inhabit. It moves us through space."

Luce's head began to hurt once more. The robots explanations continued to use terminology that he could not comprehend, but he was not prepared to give up. He could understand the concept of moving; it connected with the way his airchair functioned. That seemed like the best way to start his inquiries.

"You say we are moving. Moving where? In what?"

Gabe glanced back at Luce as he stepped down into the inverted dais of the Bridge and headed toward one of the embryonic airchairs that looked larger than the others. He seemed almost sympathetic over Luce's bewilderment.

"We are heading toward section 14 15 23 in quadrant 8 5 18 pinpoint 5. We were supposed to be on course for a planet that revolves around what you humans affectionately call Sirius, the Dog Star, but Captain Al inadvertently allowed the central computer to shift direction. Then after his, ahem, release, the central computer relegated everybody to Level Four for the remainder of the journey. None of you asked any questions. You did not care to know your new destination. You simply accepted the decision handed down to you and have followed it ever since. That is, of course, until now...until you."

Luce was stunned. The robot seemed to talk in circles, but he would not let that confuse him more. He pressed on.

"You keep talking about this Captain Al. Who is he? I want to meet with him. I thought you were taking me to him."

"I have," Gabe replied. "He is here before you."

And with that pronouncement, the robot grasped the large chair and spun it to face Luce. Seated inside were the rotting remains of Captain Al in a dark blue body suit. His eyes were sunken in and his skin was thin as parchment. The fingers were essentially skeletal. Desiccated arms stretched out like the picture on the side of Mol's airchair, and his body did not move in the way the women in the alternative Med Room did not move. Nor did he speak.

"What is wrong with him?" Luce asked flustered. He still had not come to grasp what the robot had been leading up to this whole time. "Why does he look like that and remain so still?"

"It is because he is dead, my friend," Gabe trumpeted in a particularly resonant voice. A gleam of red flashed in the robot's electronic eye and penetrated to the depths of Luce's mind as the machine repeated its word for the benefit of effect.

"He is quite dead."

Rotbody

The Life of Gabriel Part II—Trials and Tribulations

"I have been as dark as life will allow"

I was the figure of health, purity, and brilliance—six foot plus with cropped auburn hair, finely chiseled features, and a gleam in my color changing eyes. I walked through life like a fresh breeze and went wherever my fancy directed me.

The world bowed at my feet.

Forget the clichés! I snatched the photo from the nightstand, using my remaining hand to do so, and brought it close enough to my face to see it in the candlelight. The picture showed me standing upon some foreign hilltop, grimacing against a frigid wind. Theresa, my ex-girlfriend, stood next to me. Her head tilted upward in my direction, and she gazed at my face with what appeared to be sadness. It was obvious that she wondered why I wasn't enjoying the moment as much as her. She had been so simple and beautiful when I knew her. I often ask myself why I didn't love her, then. She had given herself to me unconditionally, and in the end I had tossed her away in exchange for the next thrill I could find. I regret that now, but I have given up believing in redemption.

Awkwardly, I set the photo down and shifted my attention to the large bowie knife placed nearby. I had obtained the knife years ago in a redneck shop in some southern state where most of the display blades are attached to hilts shaped like eagle or dragon's heads. I had chosen a straightforward knife with a simple, black leather handle. It still retained the mirror like sheen of well-made metal, and along its side I could see my face staring back at me. The reflected image presented me as a bloated, distorted head. It made me a monster broken loose from some dark dream.

This must be my real face, I told myself. The one society hid below the surface for so long. The one I was just beginning to recognize.

Looking up and down the knife caused me to sigh, and my head fell towards my chest in anguish. I had set the blade beside the photo for a reason. With it, I intended to commit suicide. Two slashes drawn across my jugular, and peace would flow my way after a rush of crimson. Over the past few weeks, I had been running through all the pros and cons, yet I was still no closer to making a set decision on whether or not to proceed. I simply could not bypass the possibility that some ray of hope would appear if I kept living and learning. One, pessimistic part of me wanted to believe that my situation was not correctable, but the optimistic side to my nature refused to allow that thought to take hold. A strange whispering voice kept echoing in the back of my mind that I should persist and be patient.

That voice had been with me for nearly a month.

I had only been in town for three days before locating a job as a dishwasher at a tiny diner. The restaurant was run out of the owner's house on the west side of town near the residential district, and the fading paint on its white siding tended to attract a type of local lowlife rambler, who could see beyond the building's suburban facade, but few others. It was a truly white-trash position. I did not care. I was tired of extensive, academic thinking and wanted to do little but immerse myself within basic day-to-day activity. I wanted respite from the collegiate bullshit, the purely theoretical discussions concerning philosophy, religion, and history, and wished to live and experience a side to life that most scholars could only read about in their manuals. This position, in this establishment, seemed to be the perfect beginning to my quest. It would start me upon the long road of physical living and would help me get in touch with the simple man.

And the ideal part of the situation, being that I was destitute from having paid my college tuition in full already, was that the owner offered to let me stay in a loft he had built over his garage. It was not much more than a bed, a dresser, a washbasin, and a mirror, but the rent would be deducted from my wages so that I wouldn't spend it accidentally, and the cost of this rent was extremely minimal. I would have a roof over my head, would not need a vehicle for going to work (nor would I have to insure one), and would have some cash left over to save or use for enjoyment.

Right away, I purchased a few books for those lonely nights after my shift, established an account at the bank down the block, and settled quickly into my new life as a born again salt of the earth.

At first, time moved slowly, very slowly. I spent my days standing amidst the heavy steam of the washer, throwing plates and silverware into large green containers that shot into the machine upon a noisy conveyor belt. Occasionally, hot water would splash out from the side of the machine, and by the end of the day I was usually drenched from my head to my toes. I didn't mind. The coat of water upon my body, and the clinging of my clothes to my skin, had an oddly sensual feel. Each day I tried to bask in the strangeness of this work originated bath and accept it as another experience in what I planned to be an extensive array of mundane sensations.

Some nights, I was able to frequent the larger of the two bars in town. The owner and his wife were of the rural, we will argue until we die, variety, and the owner tried to escape from her every chance he got. I immediately became his excuse for leaving. On the first night of my employment, he climbed the rotting stairs to my loft and banged on my door. He asked in a voice that expected no refusal if I would be interested in heading to the local suds establishment. Fortunately, I was in a mood to explore and did not take too long to reply in the affirmative. I changed rapidly, wanting to learn about the town's local color, and off we went in the owner's rusty blue Plymouth on what was to become a fairly regular outing.

The bar was called Willy's Pig Barn, an apropos name considering it was a large red building situated in a field off of a dusty, gravel road outside of town. Most of the patrons were southern rednecks and cowboys. The men were all hard-faced and wiry, and the women tended to weigh on the heavy side. I figured that the women had to be over two hundred pounds each, with the sole exception being Vera, the bar's only waitress, who could not have weighed more than eighty or ninety pounds. Glancing around at the rustic people and the terrible décor, I found myself disliking the joint from the start. I did not want to step into this southern nightmare, but I had to resign myself to coming. I had chosen to stay in this town for an indeterminate period of time, and that required I accept the bad, or distasteful, along with the good. If it meant hearing Alan Jackson on the jukebox and watching line dancing on the floor, then so be it. People must take responsibility for their choices or actions.

I was no different.

One thing did capture my attention, though, and enamor me somewhat to the place. In the front corner, across the dance floor from the bar sat a large mechanical bull gathering dust. I would sit with my boss at our usual table facing in its direction, and I would stare at the contraption wondering about its odd ovoid shape that was somehow rectangular as well. The machine appeared to me like some futuristic leather anachronism, out of sync with its surroundings, yet belonging nowhere else. I continued to throw back beer after beer hoping that the alcohol would provide me with some justification as to how such a monstrosity could exist, but no answer seemed forthcoming.

In the meantime, Gus, my boss, railed on about the problem with liberals and the terrible state of the nation. On our fourth outing to the bar, I interrupted him and asked, "how come no one rides that thing?"

He cocked his eye towards the east end of the building, than slowly glanced back at me.

"That thing killed Jed Farley not two months ago."

"Well, accidents happen," I stated. "Guys die in football from time to time, but they don't stop the sport because of that. We can't let another person's misfortune keep us from enjoying ourselves."

"Around here, people don't get too anxious to take risks where their life is concerned," he grated.

"But where's the excitement in life if you don't take risks? What's the point?"

Jean-Paul Corriveau

"The point is that you sacrifice your excitement in order to have a life, a long and healthy one. It's part of becoming mature. Don't you have any sense in you, boy?"

"Fuck sense!" I yelled, impertinently. "I am going to ride that thing, one way or another. Who do I have to talk to in order to get that thing activated?"

Gus stared at me like I was a newly escaped lunatic and simply shook his head; he had no intention of divulging the information I wanted. After pestering him for a while, hoping he would give in and direct me to the bar's owner, I realized that he intended to keep his mouth shut. I watched him spend the rest of the evening doing little other than moving his beer mug in an arc from the table to his mouth and back again and staring at the three indefatigable couples dancing in the open hexagonal area that made up the center of the room.

The monotony of it all made me snap.

"Vera," I cried as she zipped past our table. "Come here!"

Without hesitation, Vera sidled up to me and threw her half-covered tray of newly filled mugs into an upright position just off of her shoulder. "What do you need, sugar?"

"I want to ride that bull over there," I indicated. "What do I need to do to get it running again?"

"That bull?" she asked and gesticulated toward the front of the building. The question was unnecessary as there was only one mechanical bull to refer to. After looking at me for a few seconds and popping the ever-present gum in her mouth a few times, she finally decided to answer me with a shake of her head. "Uh-uh. No way. Nobody rides that bull. Fred won't allow it. Besides, what's a good-looking fella like you want to ride that thing for anyway? Why do you want to get hurt?"

"Let's just say I like to take risks in my life and leave it at that? What do you think if I told Fred I'd pay twenty bucks to ride it?"

"Oh no, honey, not for twenty bucks."

"Well, maybe I should talk to Fred about it?"

Vera looked at me askance, pursed her lips in one corner, and nodded her head hesitantly. "Yeah. Yeah. That's a good idea. Go talk to Fred about it."

It was Friday night, two weeks later, that I finally had the opportunity to meet Fred. The bar was packed, as was usual on a Friday night, and men in disgusting pastel western shirts, wearing huge black and white cowboy hats on their heads crowded every corner of the joint. Between them, women in frilly jeans, the kind with the diamond hole cut out of the back belt line, and beige half-shirts exposing their midriffs strutted about. I glanced at the display, now and again, from the single billiard table

16

in the place where I was currently challenging a biker with a large chest sporting the typical torn Harley Davidson gear for fifty dollars.

I was just about to shoot on the eight ball for game when a commotion broke out across the bar. The noise level dropped through some strange case of inversion, but the conversations increased. Someone important had arrived at the bar, and the people were excited.

As I looked toward the entrance, I realized why. Standing on the platform in the slightly higher than the floor of the bar entranceway was one of the fattest men I have ever seen. He stood maybe five foot four or perhaps five foot five, but his girth was tremendous. He must have weighed at least three hundred pounds. Probably more. In contrast to his size, though, was his clothing. He was elegantly dressed in a double-breasted western style jacket and pants, an immaculate white suit with black trim, and egg sized diamond rings graced most of his fingers. The diamonds sparkled brilliantly under the harsh bar lights when he raised his doughy fist to place a Cuban cigar in his mouth.

Time seemed to stop while everyone in the bar watched his grand entrance. In fact, I had trouble believing that I had been captivated by his appearance, as well, until I noticed the beautiful girl upon his arm. I would later learn that her name was Veronica, but for the moment all I saw was a nameless vision of loveliness that I had to meet.

Veronica towered above her companion due to her unusual height of six foot five inches. She draped Fred like the python draped Gautama under the Bodhi Tree, and the red scale texture of her evening gown added to the seductive, serpentine quality she exuded. I was totally mesmerized. As I gazed at the pure alabaster shine of her neck, I licked my lips over the way it contrasted the dark pitch of her hair. And when she stepped down into the bar proper, she was a Hindu legend come to life. I could not tear my gaze from her. I was a drooling imbecile with my jaw hanging stupidly open.

"That's Fred," I heard and with great difficulty broke from my reverie to discover that Vera had appeared next to me. "You want to talk to him, well, tonight's your chance. Just make sure to talk polite, you hear? Otherwise, he's liable to rip your nuts off and not think twice."

She gave me a stern look and turned to deliver some drinks to a nearby table. My hands went slack, allowing the butt of my pool stick to slide to the sticky floor, and I took a moment to consider Vera's words. Should I bother a man who exuded such power? Who knew what good old boy connections he had to amass the wealth his clothing evinced? And it was over such a small matter too. Perhaps, I should just let it drop? Just as I was about to decide against talking to Fred, I noticed that the man, himself, had paused just across the pool table from me in order to watch the outcome of our game. I saw him turn to the biker, who looked angry for having to wait on my final shot, and nod his head at some comment the biker made.

Then he turned and looked at me with piercing orange-red colored eyes.

"Hey, boy," he yelled over the din of the bar. "You think you can make that shot?"

"Sure," I replied, unsure of what his attention meant.

He glanced down at the table and surveyed the placement of the remaining balls. "You know it's going to be tough to get around that four ball. I'm willing to bet you miss. What say we parley a little wager? Fifty dollars sound right to you?"

His offer managed to increase both my excitement and nervousness. Here was my opportunity, and if I acted smart I would not let it pass. With a smirk and a sad attempt at machismo, I said, "sure, that's fine…with one exception. If I make this, I don't want your money. If I make this, I want to be able to ride that bull that's gathering dust in the corner. What do you say to that?"

My bravado must have caught him off guard because he stared at me for a few moments with an odd expression on his face. During this time, I was a bundle of nerves. Had I done the right thing? Was he going to have me beaten to a pulp for my audacity? His face was inscrutable for what seemed like an eternity, but finally a huge, predatory grin spread from jowl to jowl.

"Ok, boy," he chortled. "You've got some cajones. You're on."

I had a bit of difficulty lining up the balls due to the tense atmosphere caused by the situation, but fortunately my aim was good. The shot sunk in the far corner pocket. As I wiped the sweat from my brow, I heard the biker howl in frustration and throw down his stick. Without a backward glance, he stormed out of the bar. Fred, on the other hand, walked around to my side of the table and threw his arm around me. He seemed quite pleased with the outcome of our wager. It also seemed as if he somehow expected it, and even wanted it. He bellowed at Vera to bring me a beer on the house, and he asked if I was ready to ride the bull. I stared at him stunned. This was happening faster than I had anticipated, yet for some reason I dumbly nodded my head that I was. He simply laughed at my mute reaction, patted me on the back, and led me toward the front of the room. Around me, the bar seemed to warp and shift, suddenly. The patron's faces elongated, growing grotesque like the reflections in carnival mirrors, and it was through a surreal environment that I was guided across the dance floor towards the corner with the bull. Colorful lights illuminated the area, and their rays bounced of the gleaming leather of the contraption. This confused me. The bull looked like it had been prepared for use earlier in the day, but that could not be possible. It had been as dusty as ever when I arrived at the bar a couple hours ago, and I had just made the bet with Fred. There was no time for any person to clean it, and yet somehow it had been.

I turned to try to ask Fred about it, but time slowed down and prevented my questioning him. While I watched, the large man chuckled ominously and pulled a metal key with a star shaped end off of a chain around his neck. Ignoring me, he inserted the key into the master control box on the wall, and suddenly the machine hummed to life.

"Mount up," he laughed again, the words seeming to take form and swirl about my head. "This baby's been waiting for a new master for about two months now." He laughed a third time, a deep archaic guffaw that rose up from the bowels of his obese frame, and I staggered in place re-evaluating my decision to continue amidst this madness. About me, the eyes of the other patrons seemed to bore into my head, pressuring me to leap up onto the broad back of the mechanical bull. Their presence seemed frightening at first, but then abruptly seemed pathetic. Who were they, I thought, try to force me to do what they would not? Had they not left this machine in the corner to rot, afraid of what might happen to them if they tried to use it? They were pitiful a roving mass of boneless flesh. I would show them what it meant to be strong. I would show them how weak and sad they were. With that I became steeled in my resolve. I was going to prove myself before all of them, and I was going to have one hell of a ride in the process. With a disdainful sneer, I leapt up onto the back of the bull and slipped my left hand up under the coils of thick rope for leverage.

The ride itself only lasted a few moments. I was disappointed. It had been too easy and not very fun. Most of what I remember was trying to keep my scrotum from being squashed every time the machine bucked me. Other than that, it was just a lot of jostling. There was no adrenalin surge or experiential rush, just a lot of erratic movement.

The patrons seemed to love it, though. As I descended from the bull, a number of cowboys ran up to me and slapped me on the back. Praise and congratulations filled the air, but I barely noticed this as my attention was drawn to Veronica. She stood just outside of the bull's safety circle and obviously wanted to speak with me. Before heading in her direction, I glanced over to the control box where Fred was standing. He grinned at me, lewdly, and then turned and nodded at Veronica as if this had all been pre-arranged. His actions mystified me, but when I tried to look back at him to gain further understanding I found that he had disappeared into the crowd. I should have wondered how someone that large and important to immediately blend into a small group such as that, but I did not because at that moment Veronica approached me with a wide smile.

Still reeling from the surreal nature of the last few minutes, I let her slip her hand into mine and lead me to a booth near the back of the bar. My body followed her willingly. It was beyond controlling my actions directly, and my vision seemed to come from inside a long tunnel. Veronica turned her large, dark eyes toward me. Her steady gaze pierced deep into my soul, and as I followed her gaze into the darkest crevices of my being, I felt something begin to germinate within. How did she find this, I wondered, when I had no clue to its existence? The newborn entity moved, feeling like a sphere of energy sparking to life, and the longer I gazed into the green pools of Veronica's eyes, the hungrier it grew.

"You know," she whispered with a sibilant tongue while pressing her firm chest against my shoulder. "I've been waiting for someone like you for quite some time. You're the first person to ride that bull in awhile and live."

"Yeah," I said with a slur as if drugged. "I heard about Jed. But it didn't seem that dangerous to me. Just another ride, you know."

"Of course, it is not that dangerous," she cooed and looked at me with a strange expression, a combination of disdain and sincere admiration. "But Jed Farley didn't have what you do. That's obvious. I should have known that he never could have handled it. No, I never should have asked him to try it in the first place, but you… you tried it on your own. I sense a hidden reserve of strength within you. It's luscious. Smelling it, I really think we should spend some serious time together."

"Yeah," I stammered, a loss for words. The closeness of her body and the cloying scent of her flesh overwhelmed me. "Well, I want to be with you too. Let's get out of here and party."

"Just what I wanted to hear," she hissed seductively. "I've got some coke. We can snort it in my car and then head over to your place to fuck. Then, maybe we'll go over to my house. If you can prove you're up to the task, that is!"

EEEEEEEEEEEEEEEEE!!!!!!!!!!!!!!!!!!!!!!!!!!!!!

The red Ferrari screamed along the highway as it headed out into the countryside. Veronica slammed the clutch, flashed me an evil grin, and pushed the acceleration higher. She acted wild for my benefit, but she also tested the limits of my recklessness. I would not let her frighten me, and I threw her a twinkling glance as I laughed.

The area we drove towards was unknown to me. The townspeople had said it was nothing but open prairie in this direction, so I was unsure about what our destination could be. "Where are we going?" I asked over the noise of the engine.

Veronica shot me an evil grin and pointed with a long, crimson painted fingernail. "To my place…up on that rise."

In the distance, the land became elevated in one location. It was not a hill, exactly, but was similar in many ways to a flattened plateau with rounded slopes. Vegetation grew in abundance across the top and sides, and this seemed odd to me considering the relatively barren nature of the countryside. I was intrigued. What secrets lay within this geological anomaly? The proliferation of trees obscured anything that might be situated up there so there was no way I could even hazard a guess.

I turned back to my companion. "What type of place have you got up there?" The banality of my question punched me in the gut, but having spoken it I stuck with it.

Calmingly, Veronica let go of the clutch and rested her hand upon my knee. "Why, I've got a mansion, darling. What else would I have?"

Her reply knocked me dumb. She had a mansion. I told myself that I shouldn't be too surprised, considering the company she kept, but I had to wonder what I might be getting myself into. Glancing over at Veronica, I saw that she felt completely at ease. Her posture was relaxed, and nothing seemed sinister or out of the ordinary like it had at the bar. I shrugged off my suspicions. The cocaine must have increased my paranoia. That was all. I would just have to take this in stride and see what came out of it, because this was way too much fun to quit just when things were getting started.

For the rest of the drive, the two of us sat in silence. I watched as Veronica turned off the main road onto a rutty, dirt road that seemed to be little used. This track led us up the rest of the way to the odd plateau where we were quickly enshrouded in a profusion of elm and oak trees. All visibility, except for directly in front of us, was immediately obscured. The only breaks through the foliage occurred where the leaves did not quite press together and allowed small shafts of sunlight to break through over the road. Even the ascent up the slopes of the rise did not provide a break in the foliage's density.

It began to feel as if we had traveled into a tunnel leading to another world.

Suddenly, we reached the top. The road leveled off, and the trees grew to greater heights. With a shock, I noticed that the oaks and elm trees had disappeared and been replaced by redwoods. But redwoods weren't indigenous to this area of the country. It made no sense. The condition of the road improved as well, and its direction straightened to form a pseudo driveway for the mansion that could now be seen at the far end of the tunnel of trees. Staring at the drive ahead of us, I received the impression that the road was no longer a simple path for us to follow but was instead an arrow flying straight toward the heart of something. But what was that something? That was the question.

The silk sheets were so slick my back felt raw. I lay in the shadow of Veronica who straddled me with her legs and rocked forward and backward. She moaned slightly while spreading her fingers through her hair. It was a gorgeous sight. I couldn't help but gaze admiringly at her naked body. I watched as my hands reached up to cup her breasts of their own accord. Her breasts were rounded and firm because of the push-up leather girdle strapped around her midriff. I enjoyed running my fingers around them, circumferentially, and then pinching her highly erect nipples. The pleasurable pain forced her to press down upon me harder.

Dropping my arms to my side, I focused upon the waves of sensation rippling through my insides. I felt dangerously close to cumming, something that Veronica sensed intuitively, and to keep it from happening she fell forward and propped herself up with both hands upon my shoulders. Her nails dug into my skin, drawing blood. The sting momentarily distracted me from the friction upon my penis, but that was enough to help push back the possibility of ejaculation. I suppressed a sigh and let my head fall to the left. From that position, I could view the nightstand, and through the haze of the moment I noticed a number random items—a silver bracelet, a half-empty vodka glass, a crystal ashtray with the still smoldering orange red tip of a joint, a hand mirror carrying ghost smeared traces of cocaine.

Stupidly, I started to wonder how those things got placed there, but then my arm brushed over the double-tailed stinger with which Veronica and I had been whipping each other earlier. She had emerged from the bathroom decked out in a full dominatrix outfit, and her face had been entirely covered by a huge black butterfly-shaped mask. With a devilish smirk, she had slapped the ends of the stinger across her open palm. I found myself spread-eagled and handcuffed to the wooden posts of the bed within minutes and was soon having my clothes torn off me. Three times two, she lashed me across my back. Each stroke burned white hot before merging into one greater sensation of warmth while I struggled against my restraints. Three more lashes sliced across both ass cheeks, followed by three further ones on each leg. I turned to look at her, but she checked my motion by bringing her mouth down to my ear. Plunging her tongue in, she breathed a soft, cool breath. Shivers streaked down my spine, and I became erect in seconds.

"How would you like to whip me?" she said enticingly.

A click informed me that one of my restraints had been unfastened. Three more clicks followed in succession, and by the time I was able to disengage myself and sit up she had already assumed a tornado-drill position at the end of the bed with her knees tucked up under her stomach and her hands covering either side of her face. Gingerly, I lifted up the stinger and draped it across her shoulder like it was a thin scarf. Pulling it towards me, I stroked the arch of her back with it and then slid it into the crevice between her legs. The sight of the stinger snaking its way across her back caused the blood to flare within my veins, and the curves of her flesh aroused me to such a level that I could not contain myself.

Roughly, I grabbed her panties and ripped them apart as she had done with my clothes. I laid into her with the stinger. Slap. Slap. Slap. Three red welts rushed across her buttocks. Slap. Slap. Slap. Three more raced across her shoulder blades. Saliva began to fill my mouth. I sensed that the beast wanted out. Veronica rose up to an inclined position and twisted to plant her lips on mine. Passion took over our equilibrium, and we fell back onto the bed, our bodies entwined. The moment merged with the past and future. A timeless stasis ensued…then…now…always. It was the sparkle of the vodka glass in the candlelight; it was a black leather sheen contrasted to pale white flesh; it was Veronica's supine form appearing almost catlike in its movements; it was the electric shock of a kiss or a whip-crack; it was the metaphoric joining of sword and sheath. I felt it move all around me, a flow and ebb, a force that expanded towards infinity, dominating me, possessing me.

I was at once in tune with the entire universe. It drove me mad.

Without thought, I rolled over on top of Veronica. My cock was a piston, furiously sliding in and out of her vagina. The clapping sound of our hips reverberated off of the walls, and I found that I could only concentrate on a single image at a time—the jasmine scent of her hair, her legs crossed behind my waist, the fire burning inside of my body. Somehow, Veronica pushed me into a higher position and managed to move my hands to her neck. She gestured that I was to choke her. I registered her desire, but my mind could barely focus on any other action. I was extremely close to orgasm. Amazingly, I twisted my fingers over her larynx and squeezed. The action sent vibrations ricocheting through her form and caused a tightening of her cunt. It drove me into a frenzied state. Death, love, action, reaction intermingled. As the pressure swelled, I began to lose vision. All I could sense were my hands clenching and my penis burning. Then, Veronica reached around behind me and jammed her fingers into my anus. That finished me. A great rush flooded out from me into her, making my body become completely taut. Veronica arched her back dramatically, and her mouth emitted a wet, gurgling noise. Unbelievably, at that point, I recalled that I was strangling her. I loosened my grip, while my body lost rigidity, and I fell into her. For a while, we lay next to each other panting. My breath was ragged; her breath was raspy. Soon, my vision returned, and the first things I noticed were the violent blue marks upon her neck. The colors deepened before my eyes, growing blacker and blacker. They sought to consume my whole universe.

From here on out, the weeks flowed into one another in a misty haze of carnality. Huge quantities of food and alcohol were imbibed by the two of us, along with liberal doses of hash, cocaine, and marijuana. I never questioned where it all came from. At night, the flesh ruled the demesne with massive sessions of sadomasochism, fucking, and the occasional simple massage. Time meant nothing as we piled every sensual pleasure on top of another, heading towards some unknown apex. Way towards the back of my mind, one warring, active part of my thoughts raised alarms across my consciousness. Wake up! Where are you? What's going on? I ignored these clarion calls. I didn't care how long these sensations could last. I only cared that they were happening now. That was all that mattered...this now.

And then one day, before I could fully realize it, Veronica and I were dancing to some melodic, trudging, heroin inspired music, and we suddenly arrived at the peak of it all.

With a tenderness that I had never seen in her before, Veronica grasped my hand in hers. "I think it is time for you to visit the Chapel," she said, and a wisp of a smile fluttered across her face.

I had no idea about what she was referring to, but I docilely followed her down to the foyer, through the back hallway, across the dining area, and out onto the veranda. A cool wind had gathered, and it rustled through the trees like the rattling of a hundred dried bones before screeching its way into the sky. No moon shone tonight. Even the stars appeared subdued, and the darkness felt palpable across the land.

I shivered as we descended the marble stairs into the garden. The situation felt very strange, worse somehow than the surreal experience at the bar, and the pungent, sweet odor of the lilacs curled about me like a fine mist. The scent clung to me, somehow, in defiance of the wind that whipped my clothes about and made the flowers seem to grab for my legs, and the odor continued to increase until it became overpowering and almost nauseating. My head swam under its influence.

Beside me, Veronica's body started to take on a translucent quality. The white of her gown irradiated her form in ghostly fashion, while we walked toward the arbor, and it transformed her into a gigantic willow-the-wisp. She refused to speak during this time, and though I wished to break the silence and ask her why we were doing this, I did not. Her purpose would become clear, soon enough, and it seemed important that the wind, with its thousand voices, be the only sound to intrude during our sojourn.

Darkness blanketed the arbor, which rose up like a demon maw as we approached. It would have been complete blackness beneath the trees, except someone had lit candles every few feet to illuminate the path. I had not taken any time to explore this far back in the yard yet, all my time had been spent with Veronica who had stayed near the mansion, and I found that I was curious as to where the trail led. It did not matter that after the active, gusty atmosphere of the garden, this place felt practically tomblike. No wind penetrated between the close growing trees, and in its absence was a severe silence. I felt apprehensive entering such a still environment, but I bravely continued on. Veronica seemed unafraid, and if she was unafraid why should I hesitate?

The further the two of us progressed the closer the limbs and trunks of the trees came to be until the path was completely enclosed by convoluted mosaic bark

24

walls. The solidity of the wood seemed so encompassing that I felt a sense of dislocation instilled within me. It was as if the two of us walked somewhere outside of time and space, and I thought of that saying, "We tread where angels fear to go". Immediately, I forgot about it as I noticed that the wood of what was now a tunnel that warped and throbbed like musculature. Was it alive? I glanced over at Veronica for an answer, determined that I would break our unspoken pact of silence over this one thing, but I was stupefied into further silence by what I then saw. Veronica's body appeared to be fading away. She was slowly becoming ethereal, and as I reached out to grab her, my hand passed completely through hers. Frightened, I looked down at myself to see if I was vanishing as well, but I was not. It was only her form that was dissipating, and as before she did not seem overly concerned about what was happening.

At that moment, Veronica stopped walking forward. I noticed that we had come to a dome shaped chamber that would properly be considered a grotto were it not totally enclosed by bark and wood. Where the tunnel met the mouth of the grotto, branches stuck out in odd directions. Their jutting and contortions formed esoteric symbols and hieroglyphs, some of which I recognized like a pentangle, but most of which were alien to me. I grew uneasy staring at all the eldritch possibilities and found myself feeling puny and foolishly pretentious. Veronica turned to me with a rather grim expression, and for the first time in what seemed to be an eternity she spoke.

"This here is the Chapel, which few have found, and even fewer dared to enter. This is the source of all power. It is the center of the universe, and if entered with pure heart and trained mind it will aid the seeker to become a king above kings. But if it is entered with an experienced mind than something more might occur."

The melodramatic tone she added to her words made me laugh, but the seriousness of her gaze pierced me like a steel dagger. I clamped my jaw shut and stifled further laughter. She glanced into the darkness to her left then, and I followed her look. There, in the shadows, sat what appeared to be a vertical portal, an unframed ebony liquid mirror. It was obviously magical, but what was it exactly? And where did it lead?

"Know, now," Veronica continued, "that the future, your future, is yours to decide. You are a star and must chart your course through the heavens, but there are rules. Remember that a star that burns twice as bright burns for half as long. Be wise! Above all, be bold! I have spoken the required words."

The experience of passing through the viscous darkness into the Chapel proper was physically traumatic. My entire frame felt as if it had been forcibly squeezed through a slimy, narrow aperture, despite the fact that I had walked upright through the portal. Once on the other side, my skin tingled ferociously, and my forearm hairs lifted upwards as if there was static in the air. I staggered, weakly, in an attempt to stay standing.

Before me, a grand hallway stretched out into the distance. It was decorated with rich velvet curtains the color of lapis lazuli, silver papered walls, and a deep onyx shag carpet. It extended so far beyond my sight that I could not determine its end, but I could see a series of doors continue sequentially along its length. Every set of two doors was positioned directly across from each other, one on the left and one on the right wall of the corridor, and each door was partly covered by the drawn blue curtains. There appeared to be hundreds of doors, if not thousands.

A cough to my left startled me. I jumped and turned to find a wizened, naked man looking directly at me with shiny, green eyes that reflected my image as if I were staring into an emerald colored pool of water. The eyes were transfixing; they prevented any movement on my part. I had to stand still and look upon this duplicated image of myself. I tried to speak, but the words coagulated in my throat and blocked all passage of sound. Instead, it was the man who spoke with a half-sinister, half-fatherly smile.

"You have reached the Chapel, now, where the normal rules of reality do not apply. I sense you are nervous, which you should be." He paused here for a moment and cocked his head sideways to appraise me further. The action reminded me of the motion that a horse or dog does when they eye something to determine how it will act. "You are wondering who I am. Good. That is a proper way to begin. Simply look into my eyes and you should know. I am a host of forms, such as with Veronica. I am Veronica...or to put it better she is I. Or stated another way, we are the Chapel. And so on. It is all one in the same in the end."

He stopped talking and studied me again. I felt the blockage in my throat loosening, yet for some reason I still could not speak. Instead, I fidgeted in place, and despite my manners found myself looking down at his exposed member dangling amidst a thick patch of course brown hair. His nudity was disconcerting, but a part of me wondered why this had to be so. Looking back up at his face, I saw his smile broaden.

"Few people make it to the Chapel. You are an exceptional person to have even entered here. In one sense, your journey has ended, but in another it has just begun. I must warn you, though, that the true danger lies before you. Beyond this point, even fewer manage to survive, but the gains to be had may elevate you to godhood. It is all a matter of Will."

I expected a gong to ring after the enigmatic import of his words, but only a ponderous silence assaulted my ears. I felt a weird claustrophobic sensation set in then. The corridor reeled and shook like a bubble falling to the ground, and the walls moved in crushingly close. The man reached out a gnarled hand to steady me. Once more, I found myself staring into his eyes. His gaze help restore my balance, and I immediately felt the bubble burst. The hallway was returned to its original shape.

"This corridor is very unstable, my friend," the man said. "Its nature is constantly shifting and transmuting. You must gaze internally if you wish to maintain equilibrium."

His words made me feel like a child, and it was a feeling that I did not appreciate. I decided to avoid confronting the feeling by asking him a trivial question.

"So, if you and Veronica are the same, do you share the same name or do you have your own? Veronica isn't very masculine, you know."

"No," he replied, unperturbed by query. "My name is Virgil."

I nearly choked on my laughter. "You are named after a Greek poet. That is pretty lame."

With a condescending look he asked, "Really. And you think the name, Veronica, is any different?"

"Well…yeah!" I answered hesitatingly. His reply question stymied me. "I mean…Veronica is an average name, but it doesn't conjure up all these crazy associations between her and some figure from the past."

"I see," he nodded gravely. "Why don't you simply call me V, in that case."

"V? Like the letter?"

"Exactly."

By this time, my head had stopped spinning. I began to feel more comfortable with my surroundings, and I relaxed and allowed my age-old curiosity to return. Glancing about the hallway, I tried to establish its purpose. Nothing readily presented itself. It seemed to simply be a typical hallway with many doors leading to probably more doors. The doors were all identical with no markings or plaques to relate what might lie behind them, and no pictures or furniture stood out to break the perfect symmetry that assailed my eyes. I wondered briefly if the place might be a maze.

"What is this place?" I asked V.

"A crucible…though most of the world religions, particularly Christianity and Judaica, would erringly consider this to be an antechamber of Hell. That is one reason why we call this place the Chapel, though it is in no way connected to that type of Christian holy site. It is to offset the misconception most people have. This place is that trial by fire through which a person may enter the next higher state of existence. If the person fails the test, then they never move out from the flames. It is quite perilous indeed."

He was being enigmatic again, and his indirect responses were starting to annoy me. There were no flames around us. What was he talking about? I decided to be annoying in return and shifted my line of questioning into a more personal direction.

"Why are you naked?"

"Because I am the furthest layer in," he replied, nonplussed. "There is nothing beneath me to conceal."

Yet again, he had managed to provide me with an answer that required interpretation.

"Why are you here, then?" I asked gritting my teeth.

"Because you summoned me...though I led you here, secretly of course."

"Are you trapped here?"

"No, I am vast. The Chapel is within me, and without."

I was about ready to scream in frustration. I decided to try to trap him with one more question. "Why are you talking in contradictions?"

"Because to speak otherwise would limit the truth," he answered with a shrug of his shoulders. "Truth cannot be derived from a singular perspective or ideology. It is like the three blind men and the elephant, and the first blind man..."

This was getting old. "I've already heard that silly tale before," I yelled. "Each guy thinks the elephant is something different like a tree or a snake, but none of them are correct since they can only touch a small portion of its anatomy. I know! I know!" I did not really mean to snap at the old man, but his oblique responses were bothering me.

He seemed unaffected by my temperament.

"Yes, well, humor does touch upon truth. Of the various forms of auditory communication, it most often arises from the Self. That of course is because it generally stems from a person's fear or anger at their surrounding environment."

I had become weary of this game. There appeared to be no way to out-question him or obtain clarified answers. Then, I thought of one final thing to ask.

"Ok, so why am I here?"

He looked at me askance again and did not answer right away. I was pleased to see him pause. "Well, first," he started, "I have already answered that inquiry, and secondly it is entirely up to you to learn why. This hallway is merely a nexus to the actual rooms of the Chapel, and until you enter one of the rooms your reason for being here remains protean. Every moment of every day, you stand before myriad pathways to the future. Few recognize the possibilities they must select from; most blindly stumble down the first they come across. It is not my role to tell you how to choose a road along the winding way. You...yourself...must live and learn. With understanding, conceptual ability improves."

At last, I had obtained a semi-straightforward answer from the man, and yet having it did not satisfy me. I glanced once more at the identical doors disappearing into the distance of the hallway. Their non-descript facades still provided no indication of what might lie behind them. I had no inkling of which I should choose for my initial foray, but then a wily thought popped into my head.

Haughtily, I turned to the old man and blurted out, "I wish to go through the door at the end of the hall!"

V's reaction surprised me by turning sad at my announcement. "That is a very dangerous move for a novice such as you," he told me woefully. "I am sure that Veronica put you up to this. Her manipulations know no boundaries. Well, if that is your choice, so be it."

Suddenly, a great gust of wind blew down the hallway. It lifted me from the ground and carried me along the hallway's entire length with furious speed. The violence with which it grabbed me caused me to expect to be deposited in a heap at the other end, but instead I was gently set down in front of a large archway engraved in silver and gold. The sight of a unique threshold, excited me, and reinforced the decision I had made in my mind. I looked around to find V, to rub in my success, but he had vanished. His absence made me a bit nervous, and I called out to him. There was no response to the echoes of my voice. Just as I was about to shout out again, a menacing cloud of black gathered out of nothing in the air beside me. As it grew, smoky tendrils of darkness emerged from its sides and writhed about chaotically. They seemed to be searching for nourishment. Deep inside the belly of the cloud, twin glows of amber light burned light demonic eyes staring into my soul. A voice thundered from the darkness then.

"Enter!" it commanded.

When I refused to move in any direction, the gaseous entity began to float toward me. The tendrils elongated into tiny spears, and their malevolent intent to impale me brought a terrible fear to my mind. I backed away from the oncoming spikes and stepped under the arch into the void beyond. Upon my entering, the cloud creature stopped its forward motion and hovered in front of the archway guarding against my exit. I stood, shivering, in the cold void of a room and eyed the thing that held me prisoner. There was no returning in that direction, yet where was I to go? Nothing but darkness surrounded me. "What kind of Chapel is this?" I screamed into the abyss, and all the warnings that V had given me fled from my memory. Tentatively, I took a few steps away from the archway into the darkness. I used my hands as guides, but I felt nothing. There was a floor beneath my feet, that I knew, but I could sense nothing else. A few steps later, and I was granted some auditory and tactile stimulus. An unexpected crunching sound emanated from under my feet, similar to the sound one would make walking on dry leaves. The sound almost deterred me from proceeding, but I steeled my resolve for the second time recently and pressed on into the blackness. Within a few moments, I managed to touch a far wall with my right hand. The wall felt torn and rutted, but there was something unusual about that. My brain was unable to register the difference, but once the wall began moving up my arm I quickly realized that it was covered in insects and that the crunching noise beneath my feet had come from those insects that I had stepped on. I recoiled in terror from the wall, but it was too late. The insects swarmed up my body. Their presence caused me to snap. I couldn't control myself, and I jumped about in a frenzied state, stomping everything beneath my feet. I also smashed at the insects crawling upon my arm with my left hand, but it was useless. They simply continued to swarm. With one last maniacal whirl of stomping and slapping, the panic overwhelmed me, and I fell unconscious.

Thirty minutes must have passed before I realized that I was awake. The first indication came from the crimson haze that obstructed my vision; the second came from the subtle heat upon my face. I recognized that I was lying somewhere with my eyes closed. The bugs appeared to be gone. Opening my eyes, I found that I had been laid upon the purple divan in the north wing parlor. I faced one of the bay windows, and sunlight streamed in to frame me in a box of gold. My whole body ached.

Across the room, a heavy oak door creaked open, and Veronica entered carrying a pewter breakfast tray laden with various fruits, breads, and potables. She wore a sexy black and red kimono.

"How are you feeling?" she queried in a tone that was formal and distant like a professional nurse. I shook my head and grimaced as pitifully as possible. She simply nodded and proceeded to place some cantaloupe and strawberries onto a small dish. Then she poured coffee into a colorfully designed china cup, leaving it black which was the way I preferred to drink it.

An ottoman squatted nearby, and with a couple grunts Veronica dragged it over by the divan and sat down in it. She began to pluck the strawberries from off the plate and feed them to me. I wolfed each one down, feeling like I had not eaten in aeons, and as I consumed whatever she placed in my mouth I noticed my ailments start to lessen.

One piece of cantaloupe was particularly juicy, and as I bit into it a trickle of sweet liquid escaped from the corner of my lips and ran down my chin. Veronica immediately leaned over to lick it off, and the touch of her tongue upon my skin reminded me of the lust I had for her. My prick grew erect.

"See," Veronica said, laughing. "You are feeling better already thanks to my tender treatment. And we haven't even gotten to the good stuff yet."

I smiled to appease her, but the fact was that what she said wasn't entirely true. Some of the nausea had left me, but I was still sore to my bones. I don't know how I achieved an erection over the pain. My left hand throbbed horribly, and both of my feet felt as if they would burst through my slippers from swelling. I did not even want to move, not even to reach for the coffee.

Plus, the images I could recall about last night left me uneasy.

30

Appearing unaware of my continued anguish, Veronica looked down at my crotch and grinned ferociously at the tent it made out of my boxers. She set the plate of cast off strawberries and rind back on the breakfast tray and directly pushed her hand into my boxers through the front gap. Her grip felt wonderfully cool, but sticky from all the fruit juices. Despite it being a turn-on, I did not want to engage in this just now, and I tried to sidestep it.

"Listen, what happened last night? I can't remember because the drugs seemed to have clouded my memory."

Veronica ignored my question and pulled cock out through the gap in my boxers. Her wide mouth easily engulfed it, and the pleasure shock flattened me to the divan. It felt intense and immediate. Waves flowed across my body, their undercurrents washing away or concealing the pain, pushing it toward the lower epicenter where it belonged.

"Let's go upstairs," my companion whispered. The words hung like a leash from her lips to my ear. I had no choice but to follow her. My mental facilities ceased to function consciously. I was physically present in the moment, but little else. Around me, the rooms and corridors flowed past like dreams fleeing the dawn. How I arrived in our four-poster bed, I did not know. It was as if I had been magically transported there. No, that was not correct. I had never left the bed; I had always been there. I lay naked in a sheeted coffin, floating at the center of the universe.

"Don't worry, love," Veronica soothed, her face hovering over mine like a balloon. "All the pain will vanish. Just relax. I slipped some acid to you before you awoke. We have a busy night ahead of us, and I need for you to be in the proper frame of mind."

She sounded so confident and self-assured. I knew I could rely on her. She was aware of something I was not. I knew that she knew how to handle everything, so I would just lie back and let her weave her spell.

From what appeared to be a vast distance, I watched her perform her ritual. She leaned over the side of the bed in slow motion and snatched a shiny object from off of the nightstand. Her other hand stroked the hair on my chest. I was so distracted from the drug that I could not maintain focus on any one thing from moment to moment. Seemingly random events occurred about me. But they were meant to happen. This event was a juggernaut through time, dwarfing me, shrinking me to infinitesimal size. I had transformed into a cosmic spirit, staring out at the world through a tunnel of flesh. Far away, I noticed the creature that was Veronica smirk. I laughed, and the sound boomed loudly and echoed along the tunnel. It resounded through the surrounding abyss. It rolled across the world beyond the tunnel.

The metallic object that Veronica held came into view then. It was the bowie knife I had bought at that pro-militant store. She had unsheathed it and placed it above my chest. The sharpness of the blade hurt my eyes, and her bared teeth and dilated pupils made me uneasy in my altered state.

"Just relax, darling," she repeated. "This is just to help you be reborn. It will draw us closer together."

Her words did not sound promising to me, but once again I was unable to move or protest. The drug had kicked into high gear, and my muscles felt completely useless, nearly paralyzed. My head mobility remained though, so I looked about the room for something...anything...that might help me out. I immediately noticed that the layout of the room had been altered. Four fat candles on ornate three foot tall metal silver holders burned at each bed post, and a fifth sat about a yard or so from the foot of the bed between my open legs. With an unexpected burst of clarity, I realized that Veronica had laid out my naked form like DaVinci's evolutionary man—each candle connected to an appendage, except that instead of using the traditional head as an appendage Veronica had chosen to use my penis.

A burning sensation snapped me back to my main concern. I saw that Veronica had begun making selective, delicate slashes upon my chest. The cuts darkened and formed strange symbols, and after a few seconds the blood seeped out and created little pools of crimson around my nipples and in my belly button. Veronica breathed harder, aroused by the sight. I tried to struggle to free myself, but my muscles refused to obey my commands. I gave up when Veronica shed her kimono and straddled me with a viselike grip.

"It's time you learned the correlation between pleasure and pain," she groaned. Her face looked maniacal, and she licked her lips with an animalistic sensuality as she returned to slicing my flesh. "It'll be over soon enough, but by then you'll wish it could go on forever. Trust me. Don't fight it."

After an interminably long period of time, Veronica finished carving into me. She sighed and turned the knife towards her own abdomen. While I watched, astounded, she endeavored to cut the same lines and squiggles onto her front side that she had cut in mine. Sigils soon covered her breasts and stomach, and her blood dripped down onto my hips. She made the act look so perfectly normal, but with all the blood it caused a mental disconnect.

Suddenly, my mind found the will to speak. I raised my body up from the bed a little and forced out the words, "listen, V. What are..."

I was not sure why I attempted to ask my question that way, but I was not allowed to finish it or find out why it was so offensive."

"Don't you ever call me that, you fuck! I am Veronica. Hear me? Veronica!"

Her scream was loud enough to curdle the blood left in my veins. It seemed to become tangible and force me back down onto the bed, and I could only stare up into her eyes and watch the fury I saw crystallize into razor sharpness. In the space between us, our stares met and warred for prominence. The tension felt electric. Unfortunately, as drugged as I was, the outcome proved bad for me. I couldn't hold up under the acid's distracting influence and glanced away repeatedly. Veronica's piercing glance continued to strike upon me for what felt like ages, but finally she softened it a little. Her hand lifted up to stroke my face.

"Please be quiet, love. You're ruining the ceremony. Just relax, ok. Just relax."

Acting as if nothing had happened, Veronica dropped the knife over the side of the bed and started using both of her hands to spread the flowing blood across our exposed white skin. She began with our torsos and then when finished with them switched to our faces. For some reason, she could not help licking the blood off of my chin after she had covered it. The more she did it, the leaner her face grew. Her expression took on a feral countenance. No, consumed might be a more appropriate term. I watched her smear more blood over our bodies, and the evil behind her eyes increased.

Abruptly, she grabbed my right hand and thrust it between her legs. It came back covered in a thick, staining blood. I could see that this wasn't from one of the cuts. Then, she knee-walked her way up my body and settled her legs around my head. Her pussy sat just in front of my mouth, and a pungent odor wafted forth. Habitually, I started pleasuring her, my tongue piercing deep, my teeth nibbling her labia, my nose rubbing her clitoris and pubic hair. All the while, the crimson ichor flowed over my face and into my mouth. Its salty tang shot lightning bolts toward my brain, yet still I drank deep. My mind wanted to choke on this drink, spit it back up, but my body continued to suckle greedily.

"Ah, ah, ah," Veronica chided. She moved her hips backward, away from my head, and sat astride my legs. "We need to save some for the consecration." Arching her back, Veronica leaned over and licked the tip of my wilting cock. It sprang up tall and rigid like an ivory tower above vast plains. At this point, my cock had been the only thing not painted with blood, but I knew that it would not last. Sure enough, her hips soon began a descent toward mine. Halfway down, she paused in her motion and stared into my eyes. For the second time since I had known her, her eyes bore a strange, earnest expression. "The blood is the life," she intoned and pinched my cock between pointer finger and thumb in order to better guide herself. I felt her labia surround my penis' tip for a moment. Then, she pulled back before driving the rest of her moistness down upon me. I moaned unreservedly in delirium.

Under waves of pleasure, the horror of the situation faded quickly. It might have been the vivid color of our blood enchanting my acid affected vision, or it could have been the universal sublimation I experienced from the sex, I do not know, but either way I found myself relaxing and sinking down into the mattress like I would if I were on a waterbed.

A wave of blood rose up around me. It changed into an ocean, where I swam and touched upon everything in existence. Wait. Veronica was everything. I was the source. I was blind to all but her, and this warm ocean of bliss. Across the waves, I heard a murmuring sound like a chant. "The blood is the life," it repeated over and over. It became a sinister whisper haunting the base of my skull.

"The blood is the life."

Once more, I stood within the corridor of the Chapel. Its appearance had been altered since last I was here, and I noted that the curtains were of a gold silk now while the rest of the hallway favored various hues of red. V stood in his original location near the corner of this end of the hallway. He appeared rather pale. In fact, he looked as translucent as Veronica had in the arbor, almost as if he were a spirit fading from the material world.

Overlooking his condition, I approached him confidently and stated, "I think I've figure out the secret to this place. Its experience, isn't it? Life is nothing more than a series of experiences, and the more one experiences the more one lives."

V had trouble replying. "Well…" he began and then paused. He had to force out the following words like a stutter. "Yes…and…no." Some force was preventing him from communicating normally with me. V struggled against it, and with a crackling burst of cosmic energy he ejected the rest of his statement. "There are many types of experience, but you seem to only consider a limited amount currently. You focus much too much upon desire. With your hunger, and Veronica's misdirection, that is a dangerous path to follow. It will probably end in despair.

V's body shimmered, phasing in and out of existence like a holographic image being turned on and off. He reached out for assistance, but the distance between us magically increased. Suddenly, I found myself standing ten feet away from him instead of only two. This definitely felt wrong, and I attempted to close the distance between us again. I needed him to help me navigate the dangers of the Chapel, especially considering what occurred last time. "V," I cried but could not reach him. I found myself flying backwards through the air. Grabbing at the walls, I tried to check my movement but was unable to find a handhold. The curtains simply tore away from wall when I grasped them becoming useless. Whatever the intangible force was, it hurtled me down the hallway and through the archway at the end. The force threw me to a cobblestone floor where I lay sprawled for a time.

I did not waste much time standing up when my control returned, and I looked vainly down the hallway for V. The other side was beyond my view. V was probably standing a mile away from where I was just now. Glancing around, it relieved me to see that the room had transformed like the hallway, and instead of an insect populated abyss, I found an immense stone sanctum that looked to my untrained eyes to be the bowels of some Mayan temple. Flaming braziers adorned each wall, and they illuminated the area well enough for me to make out its entire dimension. The flames cast eerie shadows into each corner and for some reason made me think of the cloud creature. I apprehensively whipped my eyes about, but the glowing eyes did not make themselves known. If the creature was present, it was staying well hidden which suited me just fine.

Taking stock of the chamber, I saw that the opposite side had a large, one-step dais built against it. A dilapidated altar squatted in front of some ruby encrusted drapery, and upon the altar reclined the fattest woman I have ever seen. Every inch of her body ballooned out flabbily, and deep dark crevices sat between the bulges. The woman lay completely naked, and as I gazed upon her she seductively signaled for me to approach. My mind was completely repulsed by the sight of her, and yet my eyes would not look away. I tried to cover up my eyes with my hands, but my body rebelled against me.

"Come over here, big boy," the woman purred at my reticence. "I've been waiting for you."

The grotesqueness of her form belied the insincere nature of her words. She deliberately played the enchanting starlet or irresistible whore to enhance the sickness I felt, but her role-playing had the opposite effect on me as well, oddly enough. My member became frighteningly aroused. There was something about the gargantuan size of her pussy, overlapped by the massive flesh of her belly, which switched on some node in my body and released a strange new chemical inside me. It mixed with my disgust and elevated my emotions to a level of pure carnal lust. It swayed my brain into believing that this woman would be the ultimate act of debauchery and that our merging would thrust us to heights never before attained. My body readily concurred with this thought, and it strove to push me toward this vile pinnacle of sensual experience. I found myself dazed and confused, walking without conscious effort toward her as I loosened my clothes.

"That's it," she cackled and spread her legs apart to reveal the moist, brown lips within. "Come and stick that prick of yours inside me."

I stepped onto the dais and dropped my boxers down around my ankles. My penis was a rod pointing directly at the woman's groin. Without further hesitation, I strode forward and pushed her meaty, dangling legs further apart. "Stick it in me," she repeated, and I could not refuse. The pleasure came immediately, shooting lightning up my spine. I planted both of my hands upon her huge breasts and wondered at how neither came even close to covering the vastness of those protuberances. Amazingly, her nipples were quite erect instead of being the flat colorations I expected to see. At this point, my body seized control of my mind. My hips broke into violent thrusts, and a terrible screaming ripped through my head. The pleasure changed into pain and then reverted back again. Back and forth, in and out, I became delirious from the drastic shifts I was experiencing. My mind wished for it to stop before I went insane. It wanted me to be able to cum and reach an end to the experience, but some force held my orgasm at bay.

My body would not stop its animalistic motions, and my skin felt engulfed in flame.

Abruptly, the scene turned horrifically surreal. The woman's appendages began to shrivel up, growing smaller and smaller until they vanished beneath the bulbous mounds of her flesh. Where they had been only gaping, festering, wounds remained. Even her head had shrunk and disappeared into what was now a gigantic sphere of pulsing skin. I could do nothing but watch as the folds of skin also shrunk in size and tightened until it was little more than a ball of diseased encrusted holes. Throughout it all, my body continued fucking. The pleasure, pain combination held me captive, and the sensations were too intense for my body to stop.

The sphere hovered in the air and began rotating in various directions. Every time I thrust my penis forward it moved so that I pierced a different hole. I tried yelling at my body to discontinue its mad actions, but it would not. It kept thrusting and finding a new hole. Presently, a putrid liquid, like excrement, began seeping out of each orifice. My penis plunged in again and again, regardless. Some of the liquid spurted out from the holes like volcanic eruptions, and it covered my body in a dark brown slime. Still, I would not stop. I was engulfed by fire and excrement, pleasure and pain. The primal energy that had been pent up inside me reached dangerous levels. I could feel myself preparing to explode.

Then, with a burst of white light, I did.

It was in one of the guest rooms that I awoke. The curtains had been closed, and I could not tell if it were day or night. For that matter, I did not know what month or date it was either. I may have been staying at this mansion for weeks or even longer for all I could remember.

There were no signs of Veronica nearby. I listened carefully, but the mansion was as quiet as a grave. I probably should have been concerned about being alone in such a large empty place, but I was exhausted from our lovemaking and glad for a break. I pushed my head further back into the pillow and sought after some additional sleep, but unfortunately my mind kept wandering back to last night's activities. From what I could recall, the two of us had been out of control, and my entire body throbbed in pain with the memory. The scene with the knife vividly returned to mind causing me to sit up quickly and re-open the wounds upon my chest.

Before I could examine them, a sharp pain drew my attention away to my left hand. Vague recollections of its soreness, along with the stinging in my feet, the day before came to me. I wondered if I might have fractured them during our excessive bouts of sex, but try as I might, I could not recall what it might have been. I stared down at my hand and what I saw shocked me to the core of my being. The skin had swollen so badly that it cracked and oozed out sickening, yellow-green pus. Throwing back the sheets I found that my feet were in the same condition. It was such a revolting sight that I screamed in terror and promptly vomited over the side of the bed.

With a loud bang, the door to the upper hallway flew open, and a tall bronze-skinned man in tight jean shorts and a light blue polo shirt hurried into the room. "What's the matter?" he panted. "What's wrong?"

The man's abrupt appearance caught me off guard and momentarily made me forget about my hands and feet. "Who are you?" I demanded, then noticed my nudity and pulled the covers back over myself.

He waltzed over to the bedside. "I'm Dan, remember? I came by last night at Veronica's request." He grinned with mock sheepishness. "You know…to party." As he noticed my wounds, his voice trailed off. "My word," he stuttered, recoiling in terror. He backed up several steps, his hand raised to his mouth, but whatever he wanted to say immediately stuck in his throat. Finally, he blurted out, "I got to go," and fled from the room.

Of course, the whole incident deeply worried me. It became clear that I needed to remember what had gone on over the past couple days, but the profusion of drugs I had taken obscured the majority of my memories. Pain shot up my arm again, distracting me from my task. There was no point dwelling on indistinct memories anyway. I needed to care for the cracks on my hand and feet before figuring out the larger issue. Obviously, my lack of care up until now had allowed my appendages to become infected, and if I let them go any longer much more serious damage would occur.

It came to me that there was an emergency medical kit in the kitchen. Tentatively, I swung my feet over the side of the bed and attempted to stand. Dagger sharp pain dropped me back to the bed. The agony in my feet was almost unbearable. I had to turn part of my mind off and focus past the pain to push myself into an upright position.

The trip downstairs was nothing but suffering. I had to grind my teeth as I hobbled along the hall, my shoulder pressed against the wall for support. When I arrived at the grand staircase, I realized that I would have to slide down the banister on my stomach in order to reach the main floor, but from that point on the rest of the journey went easier because I was in a daze from the pain.

The medical kit proved to be exactly where I thought it was, and I rapidly pulled out the gauze and ointment. I was very liberal in applying them upon the affected sites. The relief they provided turned out to be minimal, but they would keep things from becoming worse. At least, I could relax now and think more clearly.

Jean-Paul Corriveau

I wondered about how I had received the wounds upon my appendages. I could remember Veronica cutting up my chest, but I could not remember what had caused the infected wounds. Plus, why would my chest fail to become infected while the condition of my extremities was terrible? Had Veronica done something to them that she had not to my chest, like urinated on them? No, that did not make much sense. But then again, what did concerning the prior week or so? Maybe, she had cut my hands and feet days earlier? That would explain why I could not recall the incident.

A window over the back garden provided me with a close view of the arbor. Suddenly, I remembered my dreams of the Chapel and the location's strange properties. I had a hazy recollection of Veronica leading me through the garden and into a tunnel behind the arbor to reach it. Had that really occurred? Were those scenes more than dreams? I couldn't be sure, but I knew that I needed to find out.

Walking did not bother me overly much now that my feet were wrapped in gauze. I felt pangs during changes in elevation and when I placed too much pressure upon one foot instead of distributing it evenly, but overall my mobility was fairly unhampered. I managed to reach the garden with little exertion.

Outside, the sun glared down upon me, angry that I would desecrate its precious daytime. I had not left the mansion proper for some time, except, possibly, when first traveling to the Chapel, and the brilliance of sol's rays stung my eyes. I shielded them with my good hand and looked around. The garden was beautiful. Whatever groundskeeper cared for the estate had planted peonies throughout, and the sight was entrancing.

Part of me wanted to lie down and let my surroundings transport me away from my problems, but I had a mission to accomplish. With a heavy heart, I staggered across the garden.

The arbor looked much different than I remembered. It consisted of a simple marble bench set in the middle of a small grove of willow trees. No tunnel exited from the rear of the arbor, and no candlelit path extended off into the forest. There could be no magical hillside gate, as the land dropped off in a steep decline, just feet beyond the back of the arbor. The sight perplexed me. Had our journey been nothing but a dream? Had the Chapel been nothing more than a drug induced hallucination? I could not believe that was the case, yet, the lack of physical evidence said that it was.

Contemplating the ineffable, I turned and plodded back to the mansion.

Veronica returned late in the evening. Since the mysterious Dan had disappeared, I had been alone all day, and I spent most of it resting in the parlor. That had eventually become boring, and not wanting to be confined in one spot too long, I moved across the foyer to the study as night fell. Veronica located me there reading a book on metaphysics I had found by A.C. She swept up to me, settled herself in my lap, and wrapped her arms around my neck. Her kisses held an annoying resonance that I could not identify. I tried to push her off but could not because of my hurt hand. She effected the action for me, though, jumping up heatedly.

With her hands planted on her hips, she spit, "what the fuck is your problem?"

"I'm not feeling well right now," I replied ashamed. "I've got something seriously wrong with me, and I think I should probably go to a hospital."

Veronica's arched brow accentuated her skepticism. "Oh, come on now. That's a little irrational, don't you think? Why do you need to go to a hospital?"

I lifted up my bandaged hand for her to see. She grasped it with both of hers and peeled back the gauze to examine the skin beneath. Her eyes rolled, and I could tell that she did not consider it to be a serious matter.

"This is nothing," she criticized. "Just some small cuts, that's all."

"Just some cuts?" I shouted. "Just some cuts? They're fucking infected."

"Maybe…but they're not that bad. Plus you already put some anti-bacterial ointment on them. They should heal up nicely."

I remained stubborn in the face of her contradictions. "I don't care. I want to go to a hospital."

Veronica sighed with a deep heave of her bosom. "You are not going to a hospital, and that is final. There is nothing wrong with you…besides I don't have time to take you." With a flip of her hair, she turned and stalked toward the exit to the foyer.

"Hold on a moment. I'll be right back."

She returned with a syringe and a small vial of clear liquid.

"What's that?" I asked. I was not sure I trusted her after the past couple nights.

"Morphine…for the pain. One little injection, and you will be doing fine."

We did not speak while waiting for the drug to take effect. Veronica sat in a nearby armchair and watched me cautiously. Occasionally, she would reach over and stroke the inside of my leg. I simply sank back into my plush chair and hoped that the pain would dissipate.

Perhaps she is right, I thought. Perhaps I could get by smoking or injecting the pain away until everything was healed. I could blow all my problems away in a gray-green haze. That way, the party could continue without pause.

When it was apparent that the drug had taken affect, Veronica took hold of my good hand and tugged me to a standing position. I cried out briefly as the pain broke through the morphine and my feet gave way beneath me, but I did not resist her pull. Veronica caught hold of me as I crumpled to the floor, and with a strength I did not know she possessed she hoisted me into the air and carried me fireman style to the master bedroom. My head spun crazily by the time we arrived.

Veronica threw me onto the bed like a doll. She began unbuttoning her blouse, allowing her nymphomania to assert itself again. Her passion transferred into me. Instinctively, I attempted to unbutton my pajama shirt though the pain in the fingers of my left hand was unbearable. The pain forced me to remove my clothes with one hand. I was not very successful at it, and by the time I had undone two buttons, Veronica was already fully naked and tapping her foot impatiently at my slow progress.

Instead of trying to help me, Veronica glared fiercely at me and stormed from the room. She returned with a meat cleaver clutched in her right hand. I was frightened at first, oddly thinking that she intended to murder me, but she stomped up to the bed and pushed the dangerous implement into my good hand.

"Well...what are you waiting for?" she screamed. "Do it!"

I stared up at her in confusion.

"You know the rules," she continued. "If your hand offends you, cut it off!"

Lacking mirth, I laughed at her as she blurted those words. "Who are you to quote from the Bible?"

"Bible, Torah, Koran, Vedas...it doesn't fucking matter what I quote from. All writing is metaphorical, except in those few individual instances when you live the writing. You are in one of those moments now, so just finish it. Cut the fucking thing off!"

I could tell by the set of her eyes that she was in earnest. At first, her reaction stunned me, but the more I considered it the more irate I became. Who was she to demand that I amputate myself? Who the fuck was she?

I threw the cleaver to the floor. This gesture of defiance sent Veronica into a frenzied state. She pulled at her hair and spun around.

"Think about what you are doing, you bastard! Your hand is going to hinder you from living your life the way you want to live it. Do you want to give up all this pleasure?"

Despite her irrational yelling, her words touched something deep inside me. A volatile mix of emotions battled for dominance, and part of my subconscious latched onto her false statements. This part longed to be wild and free, to release my fierce energy upon the outlying world, and it desired Veronica by my side for all eternity. And yet, this other part of me also, viciously, reminded my conscious that everything she had promised led to great pain. The self-destructive nature of the action she requested I commit was blatantly apparent. How many appendages would I have to cut off before I was left, useless and alone? Would this be the only appendage, or would others follow? I had no way of knowing, but one particular possibility seemed highly likely.

I stared at my infected hand and saw that it was beyond healing. In all likelihood, I really did need it amputated. Mentally changing tracks again, I started to sway myself into thinking that one quick chop would remove all my worries. Removing my hand would have the benefit of containing the infection, and then Veronica and I could make love again without hindrance…like before.

And yet those nagging thoughts continued to push toward the surface.

Finally, I cried, "NO," and catapulted myself off the bed. I do not know where I was headed, but I felt the need to escape from the madness in the room. I noticed that Veronica appeared amazed at my defiance, and she stood paralyzed as I stumbled out of the room and down the hall. Somehow, I wound my way back to the study without collapsing. As I entered, I dropped to the floor in front of the fireplace and lay still, feeling the cool touch of the marble upon my face. The sensation was nearly sensual, and unbelievably, considering the situation, my penis began to rise. Like an animal watching for predators, it managed to sense that Veronica had come near.

Tears slid down my face as Veronica padded softly up to me. She knelt beside my prone form, leaned down close to my face, and blew gently into my ear. The brush of her hair on my exposed neck excited me further. With minor reluctance, I rolled over to give my penis breathing space.

"Since you aren't strong enough to do this," she whispered fiercely, almost lovingly, "I will."

I had expected her to mount me and was unprepared for her true action. With a rapid motion, she swung the cleaver down and cleanly chopped off my hand at the wrist. I felt nothing at first. Only the chink of the metal cleaver striking the marble informed me that I had been amputated, but then Veronica staunched the blood with a lighter that she held against the stump. The faint warmth of the amputation quickly changed to terrible pain as she burned the wound closed. I screamed out loud, a high-pitched echo that seared through my skull and delved towards the root of my being. Outside of my body, the room spun faster than my mind could follow, causing me to start to lose consciousness. The last thing I remember was seeing Veronica rip the pajama bottoms off of my non-resistant form.

I awoke in the plush armchair that Veronica had found me in the day before. A fresh robe covered my cold form, and the end of my arm had been bandaged over to protect the stump. I stared hard at the empty space where my hand used to be. It was definitely gone for good, and yet I swore that I could still feel the fingers moving. Imagining my hand clenching into a fist sent bizarre ghost sensations along my arm. It struck me that there was more emptiness in the pit of my stomach than at the end of my arm.

A fire blazed in the grate in front of me, and someone, Veronica probably, had stacked up a chord of wood off to one side. Near the pile sat a large duffel bag. It was the bag I had brought with me when I moved to this town, and its appearance reminded me that I had skipped out on my job without warning. Like everything else, I had forgotten about it during all the partying.

Well, there was no going back now.

I wanted to search through the bag for some personal effects, but an unbelievable pain tore across my frame as I sat up. It prevented me from leaving the chair. I glanced down at my body, and the exposed flesh of my chest revealed the horrible truth to the matter. Every inch of my body appeared to be covered by the debilitating cracks that had consumed my hand and feet. As I moved, the cracks oozed out the same greenish pus that had frightened me the day before. Mentally, I berated myself. I knew that it would spread, and yet I had allowed Veronica to talk me out of going to a hospital. Could she not see that this disease would continue to devour me until there was nothing remaining? Did she not care?

Fortunately, it felt as if my internal organs remained untouched. Vital areas were intact, and that gave me the hope that all was not lost.

What I saw next nearly destroyed my optimism. A handwritten note had been left on the stand beside the chair, and it had been specifically placed for me to notice upon awaking. Gingerly, I picked it up and scrutinized the words by the light of a candle that had also been left. The handwriting was definitely Veronica's, and this was apparently a Dear John letter.

Friend,

I've left town for a while. I'll be travelling with Fred's new "big deal".

He predicts the guy will be signed to a major label by the end of

the year, and the excitement around his band is intense. I need to be a part of

that. I think I have done all I can with you.

Veronica

It was as if an invisible hand reached past my ribcage and clamped down upon my heart. I had to regulate my breathing. She was gone. What was left for me now? I felt like a worthless wreck, a rotted husk of lumber broken by the reef and washed up on the shore of a desolate island. I was cut off from the outside world, and perhaps soon that would include the inside world as well. For the first time, the walls of the mansion seemed to close in upon me, and the fixtures, which had gone unnoticed before, returned my gaze with amorphous, faceless expressions of contempt. I did not belong here, I realized. This was not my home.

Behind my eyes a flood began to swell.

The next few days passed in a mechanical haze. Every day, I dutifully cleaned my bandages and tried to rest. When I could remember to do it, I ate, but most of the time I remained in the study. There was no thought of leaving the premises. I had imagined that this place was a tomb weeks ago, and now it seemed appropriate that I would die here. I made a project of gathering all the wine from the cellar—the

French Sauvignons, some Italian Chiantis, and some Mosel based German wines—and stocking them by the armchair. I also discovered three pounds of dope in a cabinet in the kitchen and added that to my stash. Since I was meant to die here, I would do so in style.

Sadly, my duffle bag had little in it to help pass the time. There were a couple novels by the beatniks Kerouac and Burroughs, but aside from that there were only dirty clothes, a photograph of my ex-girlfriend, Theresa, and I from some summer vacation, and a couple cassette tapes with mixed music on them. My bowie knife was missing, but then I remembered Veronica using it on us during that sadistic ritual. I would locate it later in the master bedroom.

I piled everything around me like a giant nest. I did not want to have to leave the area. Walking continued to be rather painful, and I did not wish to have to retrieve this or that article from some distant room and endure the agony. I figured it was enough to have to get up and find the toilet when I needed to piss. Even then, I often decided to urinate in the fireplace so that I would not have to stagger the fifty feet to the nearest rest room. I simply wanted to vegetate in this chair and forget my troubles. I sucked down the wine in vast quantities, and I inhaled as much dope as my lungs could handle. My mind could drift off into vague dreams of better times past.

My most frequent dream focused upon Theresa. I figured that this was because I had a picture of her nearby to frequently look at. In this dream, the two of us had a glow of luminescent white. Our hands were clasped together, and the two of us traipsed across a golden plain under a comforting blue sky. We soon reached an idyllic spot where we could sit together. Her pale gray eyes would lock upon mine as we fell upon the grass, and we would gaze at each other, smiling the whole time.

This dream gave me peace.

But then I would awake from my slumber, and a violent melancholy would set in. To compensate, I would imbibe more wine. My heavy drinking made the wine become the first of my resources to run out, and when it did my dream began a metamorphosis.

It would begin in its usual manner. The two of us crossed over a field holding hands. We felt great joy in being together. Halfway to the idyllic spot, a tight knot would ball up in my stomach. Some compulsion forced me to throw Theresa to the ground, and above us dark black clouds suddenly raced over the sun. Sinister shadows crept across the grass. Glancing at Theresa, I would see fear steal into her eyes, and it would draw a dangerous wolf spirit into my body. The wolf possessed me. With a howl, I leapt upon my companion and tore the clothes from her body. I ravaged her with abandon. As I did, her grunts of fear gave way to ecstasy.

Not long after this stage of dream, the marijuana ran out as well.

Now, when the dreams did come, they were little more than fuzzy swirls of color. I maintained consciousness way too often, and the suffering I previously avoided reared its ugly head again in full force. It would not allow me to ignore the pathetic state of affairs I had embraced—the banality of living in the same room, the lack of contact with other people. I glanced about myself in utter despair.

That was when I contemplated committing suicide. I would leave the bowie knife lying on the table where I could reach it, and I spent most of my days staring at it, daring myself to take it and slice across my neck. The disease might not have been spreading any longer, but it still resided in my system. I was bereft of a hand, and any amazing feats I had previously performed would never be accomplished again. I had lived as much as I could. There was nothing left to do now but end it all.

Still, some stubborn part of me refused to give in to desolation.

My metaphorical eyes were opened the second time I read the tome by A.C. Before, the words had spoken nonsense, but now, after my ordeal, the content sounded out with resounding clarity. It was as if a trumpet call had awakened the sleeper inside me and ordered me to bear witness to the coming Dawn.

It blared...

Reveille.

Revel.

Reveal.

Revel(ation).

Knowledge will resurrect.

An army of voices joined with the tome that I read by A.C. I searched through the library about me and found other books crying for my attention. There were books by Regardie, books by Hyatt. I located novels by Pynchon, and Joyce, and Yeats. There were texts by Wilson. I read Foucault, Nietzsche, Blake, Gardner, and Camus. A legion of writers appeared in answer to the silent summons. The names of these men floated aloft on alabaster wings. They were names of power. And I spoke them aloud within my candlelit circle of light.

I cannot be sure how many days passed while I listened to their voices. My head felt unburdened by my form. It carried my soul outside time and space.

With the ability to think clearly again, I could evaluate my past. I thought about Theresa again. She had been so sweet and simple. What would my life be like if I had stayed with her? Would I be happy? I had told myself that our love was dead. I had recited to myself that we had changed during our relationship, that the person she was and the person I became were no longer compatible. I told myself that these changes would eventually bring us to each other's throat. These things may have been true, but the telling of them had been a lie. The fact was that I had been young and afraid. I had mistaken stability for conformity and love for death. Yes, I had left because I wanted to be free and explore, but I was wrong to think that I needed to be unattached to be unhindered. V had been right. I hadn't fled from death. I had foolishly run toward it, for the experience and the rush.

Truthfully, I had acted idiotically in regards to Veronica. I had imagined her as my protective serpent under the Bodhi Tree. I had equated myself with the Buddha, but my actions made it apparent I was no Gautama. Gautama's serpent had protected him because his experiences were behind him. I on the other hand had tried to ride my serpent into a pit of experience, uncontrolled, and the serpent had turned around and bitten me. I had acted stupidly Christian. I had allowed the guilt that our society instills in us to drive me to a state of depravity, and it was obvious that I was nowhere near attaining the next state of understanding. I would have to engage in ascetic behavior to move closer to the truth. It was time to stop being a blind man around an elephant. It was time to stop being a fool. I had made myself a hanged man.

But the Buddha's words offered great wisdom.

"Truth is within ourselves; it takes no rise from outward things, whatever you may believe. There is an inmost center in us all, where truth abides in fullness; and around wall upon wall, the gross flesh hems it in, this perfect, clear perception, which is truth.

A baffling and perverting carnal mesh binds it and makes all error: and to know rather consists in opening out a way whence the imprisoned splendor may escape than in effecting entry for a light supposed to be without."

A new dream came upon me.

It might have actually happened in reality.

I cannot be sure in my current state.

Veronica stalked into the room and looked about with a casual air. "I figured you would have been gone by now, but I guess I was wrong. Are you waiting for a second go round?"

"Maybe," I smirked, my smile twisted into more impish a shape than my actual feelings backed up. "What happened to the band?"

"Oh, the keyboardist overdosed on heroin, and the singer is charged with two counts of rape. I should have guessed they didn't have what it takes, but one lives and learns.

"Kind of like Jed, huh?" I teased.

Veronica overlooked my jibe and sloughed off her trench coat. She wore a black evening gown underneath that allowed her shoulders to stay exposed. Discarding her leather-strapped shoes, she slid up to me and sought to caress my cheek with her palm. I realized that she was up to her old tricks again, and despite what had happened

Jean-Paul Corriveau

between us that mischievous part of me reminded me of how long I had been without pleasure. I fought to suppress this thought. I had to bear my daily pain in mind.

"C'mon love," she purred. "Let's not fight. This can be a whole new beginning."

"No," I sighed. "Not like you expect. I need to break free from your carnal mesh." For some reason, parroting the Buddha's word did not sound correct coming from my mouth, but I needed to say them anyway. I could feel the stinging pinch its way across my body. My usual agony was reasserting itself, but for some reason the fire that typically burnt my skin was different. I could sense the flames expanding and growing beyond the boundaries of my weak flesh. They danced upon me with abandon.

In one fluid motion, Veronica stood up, slipped out of her gown, and posed seductively. As her outfit fell to the ground, I felt my devilish old desire growing inside me. I valiantly fought it, but a host of images flooded my head. They were images of passion given over to anger and dominance. They were images seeking death. Veronica faced me confidently. Her form shimmered in the candlelight, and her curves were smooth and graceful.

"Take me!" she commanded and stretched out her arms invitingly.

The flames upon my body were clearly visible now. They jumped about frantically and seemed to become energized by the conflict raging within my soul. I sought to oust the rush of dark images, but my willpower steadily weakened. In one final attempt to regain control, I rose from my hibernating den and flapped my arms upward like powerful wings to buffet away the enemy.

Pitifully, they had no effect.

A new image engulfed my mind. I saw Veronica and myself awash in a sea of blood. The image unearthed some chthonic force, and it possessed my body and forced me to throw Veronica to the ground. I fell upon her immediately. Grasping her neck, I doubled her over so that she appeared to worship some heathen idol. As she struggled against my grip, I ripped loose my pajama bottoms and freed my stiffening cock. Veronica's motions stilled as I separated her buttocks and shoved my cock up her anus. Both of us exhaled in pain at the contact.

About my skin, the flames darkened and kept me from achieving sexual dissipation. The flames shifted from blue to navy and then finally to black, and the change reminded me of the injury my choking had caused upon Veronica's neck. This could not go on. I popped my dick out of her anus and saw that the flames lightened again.

They did not return to their original colors, though.

Rapidly, Veronica whipped around and slapped me across the face.

"You asshole!" she screamed.

I knelt emotionless beside her. I was unable to react, and yet something nagged at the core of my brain. Passively, I watched while Veronica stood up. She appeared twenty feet tall, towering above me.

"You're pathetic," she growled. "You make me sick. One minute, you pander to your desires, the next you tell yourself that you have sinned and must repent. Hypocrite. Your repression of yourself only makes it worse. Why do you think you explode with this total lack of control?"

A terrible rage grew within her, and another backhand from her sent me spinning to the floor. "When are you going to learn?" she screamed. "When are you going to understand and transcend?"

Snatching up her clothes, she rapidly dressed herself before fleeing from the room. I heard the Ferrari rev up in the driveway and go squealing off down the tree-lined drive.

I was alone again.

Or so I thought.

A strange glow prompted me to lift my head and investigate. I recognized V hovering in the air a few feet away. He remained silent, but his open arms communicated plenty. It was time to return home. Through him, I had another chance for ascension. As I reached toward him, his ghostly form floated backward, away toward the arbor. "Come after me," it bade.

In my anguish, I had completely forgotten about the Chapel. I had pushed it to the back of my mind, because I had associated it with Veronica and our pleasure-pain orgies. Now, I understood that my darkness had transformed it into a torture chamber. But that also meant that I could transform it into something better. I could enter it with experience and Will; I just needed to purify my mind. The power resided within me. I did not need drugs or any other device to open the door to its mysteries. I could cross through of my own accord and find a place of strength and rejuvenation.

Yes, I would return to the Chapel and use it properly. V would be there, and he would help guide me along its corridors. Then, when I was suitably enlightened, we would locate Veronica (or Venus or Valerie or whatever her name might be at the time), and we would join together, the three of us experiencing twenty-one on a chariot of the soul. Three pairs of hands would we have (I would be magically healed by then), three pairs of feet, and most importantly three pairs of eyes—eyes gazing out upon the world from our center zone—eyes in the midst of the maelstrom, our storm, our creation, one Being.

Addendum:

"The true principle of Self-control is liberty. For we are all born into a world which is in bondage to ideals; to them we are perforce fitted, even as his enemies to

Jean-Paul Corriveau

the bed of procrustes. Each of us, as he groweth, learns repression of himself and his True Will. 'It is a lie, this folly against the self: these words are written in the *Book of the Law*. So therefore those passions in ourselves which we understand to be hindrances are nor Art nor part of our True Will, but diseased appetites, manifest in us through false early training. Thus the Tabus of Savage Tribes in such a matter as love constrain that True Love which is born in us; and by this constraint come ills of body and mind. Either the force of repression carries it, and creates neuroses and insanities; or the revolt against that force, breaking forth with violence, involves excesses and extravagances. All these things are disorders, and against Nature. Now then learn of me the testimony of history and literature, as a great scroll of learning. But the vellum of the scroll is of man's skin, and its ink of his heart's blood."

Liber Aleph, A. Crowley, 1962

The Undead

"I am the assassin with tongue formed from eloquence
I am the assassin providing your nemesis…
Unsheathe the blade within the voice"
—-"Assassing" Marillion

There are two reasons why people kill—for pleasure or for power. It doesn't matter which of the two downward paths a person walks; it always starts because of passion. A person wants to see more, feel more, or in some cases less, but it eventually comes down to addiction. The feet keep moving forward, pushing on into the deepening gloom, and with every death comes a bright flash of the beyond or a renewing of sensation. The killer walks from moment to moment hoping to reach a point where he or she can regain their long lost equilibrium, though deep inside they know they never will.

I shut the diary, pinched my eyes on either side of my nose with thumb and pointer finger, and trembled. I was in deep trouble. This woman was certifiably insane, and it seemed obvious that she intended to make me her next victim. She had slain Jack and Bill. Their bodies lay exposed to the elements back in the remains of our camp, their dried brown blood painted their naked forms and their abdomens were sliced open by knife wounds. Both of their penises had been cut off, and their bodies were arranged so that their hind ends jutted prominently into the air like the wrecks of downed airplanes. Their detached genitals had been conspicuously forced into their anuses.

Nervously, I glanced back at the hillside I had just descended. My eyes darted quickly from tree to tree. I watched for any sign that she had covertly followed my trail, and my mind imagined her hiding nearby, behind some low lying bush, waiting for the moment when she might pounce and strike me dead. Considering how quickly she had dispatched my friends (I had only been away from camp for approximately ten minutes while it occurred), I would have to continuously maintain my guard. To make matters worse, I had become lost. I hadn't crossed any roads, or even the Colorado Trail, for hours now and without a map or compass I could wander in circles between these mountains for days.

I should have grabbed some supplies from camp. I should have taken something that would help protect me from the weather, but I had been so shocked by the sight that greeted me that I had turned and fled in fright. I ran the whole morning all the way to this spot, bringing nothing but the clothes I wore and the diary I had found beside Jack's tent when I had got up to relieve myself during the wee hours of dawn. Could that witch have killed my friends because I had found the diary? I had thought that since it was so early I would have time to take a quick hike and read her book without anyone being the wiser. I had wanted to learn what kind of woman we had let into our camp, and my plan was to peruse her journal for any intimate details it might provide. Then, I would have secretly returned the book to the spot where I had found it. Simple. Harmless. Fun. As it turned out, I had only needed to glance at that first paragraph before I had learned more than I wanted to. I immediately raced back to warn my friends, but I had been too late.

Now, after having re-read the first paragraph, I found myself still wondering if my friends had been murdered because I had confiscated the one thing that exposed the demon for what she was. If that were the case, though, it didn't make much sense that she had left such an important piece of evidence in such a conspicuous place for me to find. Anger raged through me, and I grabbed a small rock and hurled it against the trunk of a nearby tree. I had no way of understanding this woman's reasoning. I was confused by the events that had recently transpired, and the tightness in my throat seemed to be the source for my need to cry. Why the fuck did that strange woman have to come across our camp? Why couldn't she have missed us by a couple of miles and ended up in that little village by the lake? Fate was a cruel little shit if you asked me. Of course, now that I thought about it, we weren't forced to let give her access to our site. I hadn't liked the look of her, but I didn't press my objections when Jack over-ruled my suggestion to send her packing. And, well, Bill always went along with Jack's wishes. He probably had visions of himself and Jack double-teaming this girl from the unknown, but as far as I was aware only Jack had bedded with her last night. At least, I think that was the case.

The aspen grew closer together the further into along the valley I tread, and the elevation increased slightly upon reaching the base of a small mountain. I figured that I had about five or six hours until nightfall. With luck, I could reach the peak before darkness came and obscured the bearings I hoped to obtain from the mountaintop. This peak looked like it had a decent view of the whole valley and beyond. I would have to be quick, though, because it would turn cold up there after dark. The light windbreaker I had on was fine to wear during the day, but it would do little to keep me warm after the sun set. The best thing would be for me to find someplace to sleep here at the base, nestled against some tree or bush with the ground foliage as a makeshift blanket, and then head tomorrow morning toward whatever destination I managed to determine from the peak.

The ascent was fairly steep. I cut numerous switchbacks across the slope and weaved in and out of the trees that seemed strategically placed to slow my climb. I found myself hoping that this was only a 12'er instead of one of the numerous 13'ers that were prevalent in the area. I didn't have much energy, and I wanted to conserve some for my trek tomorrow. If I had brought some found with me or wasn't worried about an abrupt attack from my pursuer, I might assault the slope with more recklessness and make good time. Instead, I chose to pace myself and keep a wary eye out.

Little sounds kept me on edge. I jumped every time a squirrel ran across some leaves or a hawk let out a sudden squawk. I have to say, though, that it wasn't just my fear of the girl popping up that made me nervous. This was wildcat territory, and I could just as easily be attacked by some vicious beast as by the blade of my auburn-haired huntress. I wasn't exactly eager to have either event occur.

The hike seemed to take an eternity, but I eventually reached tree-line where I stopped to take a few deep breaths and let my head clear. The air had gotten rather thin and crisp at this elevation. I found myself exhausted from anxiety and exertion, and I was forced to sink down upon a couch-shaped rock to regain my senses. My sweat had formed flakes of salt on my forehead, and the dehydration from this caused my head to spin slightly.

The mountain turned out to actually be a 13'er, so there was no chance of my reaching the peak before nightfall. That mattered little, since I could easily see the spread of the land from this height. A familiar looking peak rose up in the distance to my left, while straight ahead the smoke from a campfire curled lazily skyward from across the long valley. I wondered for a moment whether it would be my killer's fire or someone else's. I quickly determined that it wasn't since I had travelled from somewhere to my left, and she would have had to also. It seemed impossible that she could have traversed the distance to where the fire was at in just a few hours and gotten that large of a blaze burning. More than likely she was holing up somewhere directly below me at the mountain's base.

Behind me, the sun had settled beneath the mountains, leaving the sky a pink hue fading into azure. There was no time to descend the slope without risking injury. In moments, the stars would poke forth, and those clouds glowing like white fire to the west would become obscured by darkness. I would be forced to pass a frigid night huddled against this nearby, moss-covered boulder, and I decided that come morning I would immediately begin hiking towards that campfire and hopefully salvation.

A jabbing sensation along my left side reminded me of the diary that I had shoved in the large side pocket of my windbreaker. I pulled it out and ran my hand along its cover and binding. They were rough and cracked from excessive use—similar in nature to how I pictured my huntress' past. Holding the secrets to her thoughts I decided to utilize the last vestiges of daylight and read some more from its pages in order to gain enlightenment as to why I found myself in my current situation. I had to specifically know why she came after us.

My first murder occurred at a high school party back in ____. I had been in love with the local heartthrob, Ian Mckellan. He wasn't a burly athlete like the other boys in town, but he had a fiery red Chevy truck and an exciting, adventurous attitude that had all the girls seeking his attention. I felt that I was the only one worth his time. Somehow, I knew that if he talked to me that I could prove myself better than all the other girls. I made sure that I always smiled and said hi to him when we passed in the hall. At football games, I managed to sit near him with my girlfriends and laugh a lot to get him to look at me. I always stopped to buy a shake when I saw his truck parked at the Burger World. I did everything I could to get him to notice me, and then suddenly it paid off. I was at a party near the Ryker Farm in the old abandoned barn. I had gone because Ian was supposed to show up, which he did, and he came and sat beside me at the fire blazing off to the side of the barn. He told me that my hair looked beautiful in the firelight. I blushed and tried to cover it up by turning my head and running my hand up my face and through my hair. I hadn't expected him to approach me in this way. We talked for hours, with him occasionally wandering off to grab us a beer. He told me how he had been watching me for a long time and how he had been wishing we could go out. My head spun from it all. It was just what I wanted to hear, everything that I prayed for before slipping under the covers each night. I was so swept up in the moment that I didn't think when he led me out under the trees. He leaned my against a thick, gnarled trunk and kissed me ever so softly. His hands rubbed my hips and back, and I arched a little in order to accentuate my breasts. Pretty soon we were laid out on the ground making love.

For the next week, I saw his face everywhere I went. I made up plans for our next weekend together and busied myself with writing his name throughout my notebook. My teachers got angry for some reason. I just ignored them and continued my dreaming. It took forever for Friday to arrive. The situation was perfect. Jed's parents were out of town, and he was throwing a party at his house. Of course, Ian would be there. I spent hours picking out the perfect blouse, and, well, all my jeans looked good on me. I wanted him to see nothing but me when I entered the room. I wanted to command his undivided attention.

The party was already underway by the time I arrived. The family room was filled with people drinking and talking. Ian didn't seem to be present, but Kathi Lee told me with a smirk that he was around somewhere, so I walked out the back of the house and found only a couple of drunken boys throwing rocks into the pond. I headed back into the house and up the stairs to the second floor. The first door to the left was cracked just a little, and I could hear sounds emanating from it. I walked up to see who was inside and was greeted by the worse possible sight I could imagine. The room was lit by a number of candles, and there upon the floor were Ian and my friend, Sandra. Their bodies were naked and rutting. I was completely stunned. It couldn't be possible. It shouldn't be true, yet there was the proof before my eyes. I must have made a noise because both of them turned to look at me. Ian jumped up, but his reaction wasn't quite what I expected. I wanted him to shower me with apologies. I wanted him to beg for forgiveness so I could refuse him any mercy and hurt him as much as I was hurt now, but he seemed un-phased. Instead, he smiled at me. Smiled! He told me that there had been nothing between us. He said that it had been nothing but a fuck and that I had been a fool to think otherwise and that I should just go back downstairs and find some other guy to sleep with. He smiled while I crumbled inside and then he tried to push me out of the room. I couldn't believe it, the bastard! Who was he to grab me like that, after what he just did? He had no fucking right. I fought to get free, but he tightened his grip and kept pushing. I was furious. I screamed for him to let me go, but he wouldn't. He kept pushing until I managed to grab a metal piggy bank from the bureau next to the door and smash it over his head. He fell to the ground clutching his face. I didn't let up then; a rage had overcome me. I bent over him, beating his skull repeatedly with the bank. Sandra tugged at my arm and cried for me to stop, causing me to turn my fury on her and beat me the same way I beat him. I kept striking until she lay as motionless and bloody as he did upon the carpet. Then I flew out of that house, and town, for good.

My whole body ached. I was coughing violently by the time morning arrived. Tenderly I stood up to stretch the stiffness off my bones. The morning was gorgeous with the sun sparkling across the mist in the valley, warming the slopes, warming the slopes, and despite the severity of my situation I couldn't help but feel some slight sense of serenity from the view.

I strode over to the edge of the cliff where the stiff breeze pushed my hair back in streamers behind my head. I stretched my arms out to accept the loving rays of sol, and I imagined myself careless and free, heading towards some indistinct utopia with a blooming white flower in my hand and a canine companion at my heel. From this height, here on this mountain before the majesty of creation, life seemed to have returned to some distant beginning where everything had been simple and innocent. I felt as if I had reached some focal point in my existence. When I walked down off this promontory, I would be experiencing the world anew. Overnight, I had become clean and malleable, a molten ore ready to be fashioned into some enchanting form. I simply needed to reach a base point and let nature fashion my shape as it willed.

Jean-Paul Corriveau

The smoke from the campfire of last night had disappeared from the horizon. I had no set marker to guide my way, but the memory of that curling spire's location burned in my skull. I set off down the mountain at a rapid pace, feeling oddly free of all worries. Even that nagging voice in the back of my skull seemed to tell me that my dark pursuer wouldn't find me now. Phoebus' chariot had brought a new day to the planet, the sky was cloudless, and salvation sat just across this valley.

Unfortunately, my elation did not last. After only a couple hours into my hike I found myself stopped dead in my tracks by a terrible vision. A cross had been erected out of two long branches, and it stood mockingly in the middle of a clearing ahead of me. Jack's flannel shirt hung upon it, and the arms of the shirt were tacked into the cross piece to form the image of the crucifixion. Where the INRI sign should be was hung a note written in blood. It simply stated, "You're next!" I spun about in panic, sure that my predator would immediately attack me in this open space, but no sign of movement caught my eye. I kept glancing about seeing nothing. The motionless trees seemed to be laughing at my fear and frustration, and the pressure was enough to drive me mad.

"Where are you," I wanted to scream.

I loped out of the clearing at a wary pace thinking that no matter how free or protean something might seem there would always be connections to the past. The aggravating conclusion was that there would always be some intangible progenitor bearing subtle or direct influence on the current situation; a person had no means by which to completely control the formation of their life. Around me, the foliage seemed too concealing and dangerous. Every bush and every tree held the possibility of a hidden presence that could potentially do me wrong, and I felt prepared for my huntress to jump out from behind any one of them and carve my body into a portrait of oblivion. I had no choice but to carefully watch in every direction as I slowly progressed along the valley.

At some point, I reached the top of a small rise. The foliage dispersed, providing a fuller view of the land, and up ahead I saw my huntress perched upon a rock about a half mile away. The relief from the release of all my pent up anxiety flooded through me and reminded my body that I had expended all my energy, including what I had in reserve, so I plopped down in front of a small boulder to rest. Hopefully, she hadn't seen me when I emerged into the open. From the motionless state of her body, I assumed that she hadn't, but that didn't necessarily mean I should forego precaution. I continued to study her as I relaxed, curious about what type of creature could so callously kill two people and torment a third and was granted only inconclusive information. She appeared to be in deep thought. She crouched, gargoyle-like in an attack position, and she maintained her stance like some eastern Zen master focusing intently on the vastness of eternity. I took this opportunity to glance about myself. A small pool of water congregated in a trench nearby beneath an egg shaped boulder. The glistening wetness of the liquid on rock made me realize that a terrible thirst tore through my entire body, and I eagerly dragged myself over to the pool and scooped up handfuls of the brackish liquid while forcing myself to ignore the possibility that it contained harmful pollutants.

When I felt quenched, I glanced back to the spot where she crouched. The woman hadn't even shifted her stance. Looking at her, I wondered if she hadn't lost some of her human nature. As far as I could see, she acted more feline than feminine and more feral than fanciful. I couldn't help but feel some attraction to this wildness of hers. I recalled how little she had spoken the night before and how her gestures exuded carnal emotion. The thought stirred something inside of me; something that I wanted to ignore considering the situation. This woman seemed hungry. She betrayed an insatiable appetite for life, and death, and I doubted at that moment whether anything in this world would be able to satisfy it. It was a realization that struck me hard. She must have killed Jack and Bill because they were unable to provide her with total release. It seemed obvious to me that because of this hunger she would destroy anything that was unable to provide some sort of dissipation for her.

I stopped and thought about my position on this hill. I should be safe up here for some time at least. My persecutor appeared as if she wasn't going to move any-where in the immediate future, and I figured that I would be able to react before she could leave my range of sight or even reach me should I lose her for a second or two. I pulled out the diary and opened it to a random page near the front. It didn't make sense to me that this woman, hell any woman, could be so calculated a killer. I needed more insight into her psyche before I could make a positive analysis of her, and the only thing that could provide that for me was this book.

I met this guy in the greyhound station in St. Louis. He was short and dirty, and he wore this torn, light-grey sweater above some completely faded jeans. He was the type of guy that generally went unnoticed, but I noticed him because he stared directly at me from the moment I entered the station. His gaze never faltered, and I received the impression that he could see right through me or had supernaturally obtained dark secrets about myself. It unnerved and excited me a little, and I decided to approach him.

Jean-Paul Corriveau

His mouth broke into a smirk as I stomped up to him and stopped with an arrogant thrust of my hips. He seemed prepared for this action. His head turned up, and he gazed at me with deep hazel-gold eyes. They were pools of unfathomed depths. Looking into them, I almost failed to maintain my composure, but I bolstered my front and focused intently upon his mouth. I stood stock still and said nothing.

After a few moments, he invited me to have a seat. I complied and asked for a cigarette as I did. He pulled out some Marlboros, stuck two in his mouth, lit them both, and then handed one to me. I glanced furtively at him as I took a drag. His eyes never left my face.

He broke into an anecdote about this time when he passed through Washington D.C. He mentioned how he had gone outside the local station for a smoke when he found himself approached by a skeezy black guy in torn camouflage pants and an old army jacket. The guy pulled out a long silver gun and pointed it at him. Musty reefer odor billowed from the black guy's mouth, and one tooth had been covered with gold plating. A star had been carved on the tooth. It gleamed under the light of the streetlamp. The black guy had robbed him of all his money and then backed off into the night. The gold star was the last thing to disappear, fading out like the Cheshire cat's evil grin in Alice in Wonderland. *My newfound friend explained how infuriated he had been to have been caught n that situation, completely defenseless.*

He went on to tell how he staked out the station for two weeks after that night. He hid in the shadows watching patiently for the guy to return, and finally when the guy did my little friend stalked the guy until he entered a dark alley some blocks away from the station. At that moment, he approached the guy quickly asking, "Do you remember me?" The guy had looked at him wildly and cried, "What the fuck do you want?" Upon hearing that, my friend whipped out a bowie knife and opened the guy's jugular with one fast slash. The guy fell to the ground under a barrage of kicks and stomps, and my friend continued this beating until the guy stopped moving.

I was stunned. I couldn't believe that he was telling me this. And yet his face continued to look calm and detached as if he had performed no worse action than cross the street. His eyes still never wavered from mine. I couldn't explain it, but I suddenly felt this odd connection with him. Somehow, at that moment, I could tell that he knew I had also killed before.

"It's all about death," he said, a mischievous smirk crossing his face. "Life is nothing without death—both literally and figuratively."

He grabbed my arm abruptly and led me out of the station. We walked around back to where some out of place vegetation hid us from the street. I was a tumult of emotions. The two of us fell against the wall, our forms pushing together, our lips pressed tight, and within seconds he had unbuttoned our pants and maneuvered inside of me. Our rutting echoed like a beating drum. Visions sprang into my head. They merged with our rhythms. I saw myself striking Ian repeatedly with the piggy bank, and my blows landed

56

in sync with every tribal pelvic thrust. I also imagined myself killing the black guy. My friend's kicks joined the rhythm as well, and a veritable symphony of destruction played in my mind. It transported me into a realm of feeling that I had not experienced before, one where I felt myself losing hold of my control.

My friend seemed to understand what I was thinking.

"Makes it better, doesn't it," he grunted. I watched distantly as he pulled out a long knife from under his shirt. "This is what I killed that guy with."

I looked at the blade. It was amazingly clean. . .and very sharp. I would have sworn that it had never been used before. He placed the knife in my hand and returned to our sexual antics. I tested the grip of the knife. It felt cool and smooth. . .and comfortable. I put the sleek pommel to my face and rolled it across my skin with a massaging motion. My friend seemed to like that. His thrusts grew faster and deeper, and I soon found myself tingling all over. Then, something inside of me took control. With a devilish grin, I slit his throat like he had the black guy back in D.C. My friend didn't seem surprised, but his body broke into spasms forcing me to hold him tight. The ecstasy was greater than anything I had previously felt. I was still tingling, even after I had noticed him sprawled on the ground, glassy-eyed. Then it all faded. I felt emotionless and semi-dead. Kind of like those zombies or vampires in the B-grade movies that are always searching for food but never becoming satisfied. I realized that this had been how I had been feeling all my life, and I began to worry that I wouldn't ever be able to experience any ecstasy again. It seemed at that moment that something inside of me had been lost or changed forever. I had touched the root of existence, and now I was stuck between life and death, between Heaven and Hell. I would probably be unable to escape from this limbo that I could now recognize in the world about me, but I knew that I had to try. I had to continue to be alive.

Of course to do that I needed to keep my friend's blade.

I glanced up to see that my predator had disappeared from her position on the rock. I had gotten too involved in her writing and had not noticed her leave her meditative spot. I jumped up in fear and cast a number of quick glances about the area. She wasn't anywhere in my immediate sight. Suddenly, a blow sent my sense reeling. I spun to the ground at a tremendous speed, the diary leaping from my hand to go arcing out over the nearby ledge and vanish into the trees below.

"Get up, boy!" echoed from over my shoulder. I slowly pushed myself up from the pebble covered earth and rotated in position. She stood where I had been reading. Twigs stuck out of her unkempt hair which fell in disarray around her mostly covered face. Her clothing was torn in numerous places exposing smooth tan skin beneath, and the tears were just large enough to reveal seductive curves of breasts and thighs.

Black mud or dirt had been smeared across her face; she had circled some of it around her eyes so they appeared like the sockets of a human skull. The sight of her untamed nature caught my breath. I started towards her with a staggering motion until I saw the rock in her hand. She stood poised to strike me again, a vicious grin across her face, and her aggressive stance halted my forward momentum.

"What's the matter, boy? Afraid?" Her leer was infuriating, but I felt too dazed to respond.

She continued speaking to me. "I'll let you in on a little secret…something that most of the masses refuse to admit. It's not my evil that terrifies you. It is the exposure of your own weakness. It is the unveiling of your repressed desires. You want to kill me right now, but you are too afraid and weak to do so. You are too afraid of your own potential."

Her words spun around my head, while the earth spun below my feet. My brain was finally starting to register the blow she had dealt me with that rock. As it realized the damage I had sustained it began to shut down. An inky darkness overpowered my vision, and I fell to my knees with a final view of her staring at my dizzy stumbling form. The gleam of her grin burned strongly into my mind, even after consciousness left.

I awoke some time later with the sun preparing to set. I was laid out on the same rock I had passed out on, and my head throbbed violently. A splashing sound to the right drew my attention. My persecutor stood in the pool of water, bathing. She had she her ragged clothing, and she splashed stagnant water across her bare chest and arms. The sight stole the breath from my lungs. She was a vision of Artemis in the hidden glade, and I was the fortunate (unfortunate?) mortal allowed to spy upon her.

Her hair cascaded down the front of her face, covering her features and hiding her expression. She seemed to be the perpetual mistress of concealment, and in spite of her naked form managed to keep her Self unrevealed. I realized then that I had not yet gotten a good view of her and that I had never really been able to stare into her eyes. The night she came into our campsite it had been very dark. She had kept well away from the fire, and her features had been obscured by shadow. Even earlier, when she struck me with the stone, the mud on her face had veiled her appearance and made her look like some animated grim reaper of the forest. I focused intently as she washed herself, hoping to catch a glimpse of her true features, a difficult task considering the distracting nature of her nudity. Fortunately, she had yet to notice I was awake, and I was able to casually observe her without her knowledge.

After a few moments, she walked over to a backpack I had not seen before and pulled out a pair of jeans and a t-shirt. She donned these quickly and then stepped into some hiking boots. It disappointed me that I couldn't view her exposed body any longer, but I had been provided with a minor revelation. She had the ability to transform herself. Intelligence, as well as a civilized quality, existed within a person that up until now had appeared to be nothing more than a vicious beast of the wilderness, acting purely on instinct and desire.

The girl busied herself with starting a fire in a little hollow in the rock. She began with a little teepee of kindling wood, blowing softly to get it lit, and then once it flared up added slightly larger branches, one at a time, to increase the size of the blaze. Darkness began to settle as she worked. I took the time to glance around and view my surroundings and felt surprised that the mountains seemed extremely peaceful and calm. Everywhere about me, small rustling sounds proved that the various animals of nature were going about their daily routines as if everything were normal. It didn't matter to the rest of the world that I might be about to die or that I had been through such duress recently. Life went on.

I looked back at the girl as she continued to feed the blaze. She seemed unaware of her immediate environment, and she didn't even notice when a magpie landed on a small rock beside her. It had a lustrous color to its wings; the indigo appeared more purple than usual, very deep and regal, almost velvety, and the black was thick and shiny. The white of its breast, too, seemed unnaturally pure. It was as if the bird expressed the perfect and absolute synthesis of opposing elements, and while I watched it cocked its head and stared directly at me with one large glassy eye. I thought that maybe it wanted to communicate. Up rose its long thin tail. It pointed toward the setting sun. Its message was confusing. I sat up to study it closer, barely noticing that the girl stared at me for a second before returning to her work. The magpie paused for a few moments, than cocked its head again to stare at me with its other eye. The tail shifted position of its own accord, and it pointed now toward the ghostly harvest moon which had just started its ascent into the sky. The sight of the juxtaposition of these two distinct celestial bodies activated some dormant part of my mind. I felt an electric tingle flow from groin to scalp in connection with this mysterious symbolism, and yet, despite my physical reaction, I remained unsure of what it was supposed to mean.

"So, you are awake."

The sound of my tormentor's voice startled me and scared the bird into flight. I turned to look at her and found that she was staring directly at me. She had the fire burning fiercely beside her. Unfortunately, her hair continued to cover her face, and I was unable to satisfy my curiosity concerning her features, though I could see the glint of the firelight in her eyes. They gazed straight through to my soul.

"How long have you been watching me?" she cooed. "Did you happen to see me bathing?"

I watched as she sidled away from the fire and moved closer to my position. I wanted to say something, but the words struck in my throat. They formed a large viscous ball that lodged directly behind my Adam's apple and defiantly refused to budge. I was forced to watch her serpentine approach like a helpless rodent.

"I bet you're wondering why you are still alive. Well, don't worry. I've got plans for you. Of that you can be sure."

She sat down beside me and sensually ran her hand across my cheek. She treated me like a lover, and my body, rebel against my frightened mind, responded to her caress. I felt a stirring in my loins that would not be denied. The truth was that I had been foolish to observe her so closely, seeing her naked and splendorous, and now that I had viewed her as more than some maniacal killer, now that I had witnessed her feminine attributes in their exposed glory, my mind lied to me about her potential motives. I felt that it would be worth risking death in order to partake of the delights she had to offer. Her physical display captivated me. It caused me to overlook the fact that she had already injured me and slain two of my friends. My newborn lust made me stupid and dull.

She seemed to sense this because her hand moved down between my legs and grabbed my crotch. She murmured and purred like a cat, and her stroking my genital region aroused my desire. I started to get worked up to a fever pitch, when she suddenly stopped her seduction and moved back to the fire. Subconsciously, I understood that she was attempting to manipulate me, but my body still screamed at the loss of her touch.

"Ya know, I've seen a lot of different places and a lot of different people. I've been from one side of this nation to the other, and the one thing that I've seen that crosses over all boundaries is that people can be coded by their relationship to desire. Some people, like me, give our desire full reign. We are fatal and free, and, I believe, the only people who are really sane. The other people in this country hide their drives behind their jobs or religious fervor or whatever. They tell themselves that those feelings are wrong or impure or even non-existent. All they are really doing is lying to themselves and creating neurosis and psychosis. These people try to make automatons out of themselves, repressing their emotions until their subconscious begins to explode into their dreams, and they can't understand why they feel so much stress, or have suicidal children, or move from divorce to divorce, or have to take the psychotherapeutic drugs that their psychiatrists prescribe. It's pretty sad really."

She hung her head as she finished her diatribe and stared at the fire with what I guessed was a melancholic air. Many moments went by before she raised her head to look at me and ask, "So which are you, the type of person who follows their heart or the type of person who follows others?"

I gawked at her for a second. She seemed genuinely sincere with her question. That confused me greatly.

"You don't seem to be anything like what I read in your diary," I said.

She laughed, "People always attach their own concept of the universe to what others write. Stories or memoirs mean what the readers want them to mean, not necessarily what the author intends for them to be. You probably think of me as some psycho bitch because of what I did to your friends."

"Well, your actions reinforce that don't they?"

She laughed again at my audacity, a deep rooted bellow that echoed through the hills around us. "I guess they do. I like you boy. You crack me up."

Her reply my head confused me further. How could she imply a kind of blamelessness to her actions? How could she laugh at my obvious disdain for her deeds?

"Ya know," she continued while stirring the fire with a short, thick stick, "I've spent a lot of time reading these past couple of years. When you are travelling alone, you have a lot of opportunity to immerse yourself in books. You learn things from the past as well as from the street, and the main thing that I've learned is that free expression cannot really occur within a society. The system forces you to repress your desires. It makes you conform to arbitrary standards and causes you to lie to yourself. Sartre showed that collective experience is a crock of shit. Trying to act based on the regulations of a social body automatically suppresses natural instinct. It is a lifeless endeavor and disconnected from the Self. From what I've learned, the only way to escape this living death is to break all ties. Sometimes you have to kill to maintain this freedom."

I looked at her incredulously. She was making some amazingly powerful statements. The initial lines that I had read in her diary sprung to mind, and they seemed to contradict her words here. Careless of my precarious situation, I decided to test her.

"You said in your diary that you feel lifeless and dull, that you need to keep murdering in order to raise yourself out of some zombie-like state. It seems to me that you are acting as much like an automaton as the masses you criticize. You also mentioned that murder arises out of passion. You murdered that boy, Ian, because he denied your affections. But now you say that murder comes from fighting for freedom which is a more intellectual endeavor. Which is it? It can't be both! You are trying to argue two opposite positions!"

She laughed louder than before at my words and even rolled over on her side like she was in pain. I couldn't grasp the reason for it. "You are so naïve, boy. Like every other mundane you need to categorize...systematize...and generalize. I hate to tell you this, but things in life are not mutually exclusive. Life is grey, not black and white. When I wrote that stuff about Ian, I was too young and inexperienced to realize that it wasn't just Ian's insensitive player attitude that I was reacting to. I was reacting to the demands of a superficial society, a society that I actually believed in at the time. And those demands told me that I was only important if I dated the local stud. Those demands forced women to become objects and toys for men to use. It wasn't just Ian I killed but the weakness that had been bred inside of me. Is it clear to you now?"

Pausing, she let the vehemence that was building inside of her to subside. I knew that it would be foolish of me to interject when she was in such a worked up state of mind. Not that I had anything worthy to reply. Her words had started me thinking, and my head spun with a multitude of new thoughts. I allowed a few minutes to pass before I replied to her.

"So," I tentatively started speaking, "you defend murder as being a natural right. As a society you believe we should allow it?"

She stared at me, and I could see that she was greatly annoyed and exasperated by my question, but she worked to suppress these feelings as she judged my words and stance against my body language. Sighing, she started lecturing me again.

"Right and wrong are merely superficial characteristics of the universe, if they even really exist at all. Right and wrong, good and evil, are social constructs, and their nature depends on which society or system you belong to and during which time. I once believed in right and wrong. I once thought that the system knew all the answers and contained the ultimate guide to how to live one's life. Then I began performing certain actions that felt natural but went against society's rules, and I was able to see that they weren't wrong at all. Those rules that everybody follows arose out of the fears of some anonymous person or people from long ago. Or they were created by those people in order to allow them to maintain their power over others. System based regulations destroy each individual person's ability to act and think on their own. These regulations force people to become machines. You have to understand that right and wrong are malleable concepts. They should only be determined at specific moments and should not be transferred between those moments. A person needs to constantly analyze their actions to see if what they are doing is right for them. It is not an easy process, but then again existence never is."

She stopped to see how I received this clarification. Apparently, she decided that I hadn't quite gotten the gist of her speech, so she resumed in simpler terms.

"Let's put it this way. You have a mob boss in New York. Over the years, this boss brings about the death of numerous policemen and rival mobsters. The boss manages to accumulate an amazing sum of money during this time, and upon realizing that he has more than he can possibly ever use he goes legit and begins donating large amounts to charity. His donations help to save thousands of lives. I pose this question, then. Can you separate the good from the bad in this situation? And if you had the opportunity, knowing what you know now, would you take the boss' life early in his career in order to save the lives of all those policemen he had killed…because in doing so you might possibly sacrifice the lives of those cerebral palsy victims or cancer victims that his donations helped to prolong? And in doing so, would you not have committed an evil act yourself? Is murder not murder, if you believe you are acting out of righteousness? Would you care to justify those Christian soldiers who walk into an abortion clinic and start executing everyone inside? It starts getting pretty convoluted, huh?"

I avoided an immediate reply and gazed into the fire, unsure what to think. She had managed to make me a little less confident about my view of the world, and as I pondered her philosophical argument the flames slowly died down. Soon, there was only the devilish, crimson glow of the heated embers. A noisy silence floated down upon our scene where the crickets chirped their white noise and the fire occasionally popped out a miniature orange fireball into the air. My captor had apparently tired of talking. She squatted by the fire with a stick in her hand, deep in thought.

For a brief second, I considered running. It would be fairly easy to escape now. She was distracted and vulnerable, and all it would take for me to get away would be to rush her, push her into the fire while she was caught off guard, and then bolt into the darkness. But I realized that part of me didn't want to do that. I actually found that I had enjoyed sitting here, listening to her proselytize, and studying her form. Her words had touched upon some deeply hidden recess of my mind, and I was determined to understand why this dormant mental region had suddenly activated and why I had never noticed it before.

A chill settled upon the area, the sphere of warmth emitted by the fire receding as the flames continued to decrease in size, and I began to shiver from the change. My captor seemed to feel the effects worse than I. She vigorously rubbed her arms and legs and kept breathing into her hands every few minutes. I proffered a stupid question.

"Are you cold?"

"Yeah," she grunted and stirred up the fire some more with her wand like branch.

This strange tingling inside my throat pressured me to continue my absurdities. I shifted my seating upon the stone and coughed a few times. Unaware of my nervousness, she poked at the embers. I coughed one more time than said.

"You know, it's probably going to get pretty cold tonight."

She remained quiet as she stood up and slid over to me. Snuggling up close, she whispered, "maybe." Despite the apparent fact that she had been walking the wilderness for days, she managed to maintain an ancient, sweet smell of jasmine. Her proximity overwhelmed the rationale side of my mind again. Instinctively, I wrapped my arms around her waist and pulled her nearer. Her body melted into shape with

64

mine, and our connection heightened all the sensations I felt at the time, the firm and cool pressure of the rock on my back, the warm and soft curves of her hips and chest. My fear of her completely disappeared. Here…now…she was just another person. She was a girl who nature around a passion in me, and her nature was a mystery that I intended to unveil. My hands began stroking her back and buttocks. It was a simple method of foreplay, but standard, and she responded positively to my manipulations. She ceased being the psychotic murderous and changed temporarily into a tender lover.

We made love through the witching hour, undoing just enough of our clothing to allow us to join, and by the time we were done we no longer felt the bite of the night air. We lay upon the rocks, curled up in each other, and we stared up at the multitude of brilliant holes poking through the sky. Everything felt timeless and proper. Our worries seemed far away.

I suddenly recalled an unanswered question I had earlier.

"What's your name?" I asked. "Now that we've been together I think I should know."

Silence responded. I lay patiently while she held her tongue and worked over the situation in her mind. Just when I felt that she was not going to answer me, she meekly stated, "ya know, to have something's name is to have power over it."

"What does that have to do with anything?" I blurted. "My name is ____." Again, I was a little confused by her reply, though this time I was angry as well. "I want to know your name. We just made love."

She nuzzled against my shoulder after I emphasized that last point and appeared to ponder my question. I held still and waited calmly for her to say something. I thought I could see the sky lighten to the east by the time she decided to humor me.

"It's Lilith," she said, her voice barely audible. "Lilith."

With that I was able to fall inside myself and plunge into sleep.

Most of the morning had passed by the time I awoke. Lilith had left my side, and the absence of her body had slowly stirred me from my slumbers. I gingerly moved myself into a standing position and stretched toward the gentle sun. One knot on my left shoulder blade refused to unwind; the painful pulse of its tightness reminded me that a person should never relax in an uncomfortable position. While contemplating my aches, I suddenly noticed a stinging sensation emanating from my right palm. I looked down to see that an encircled five pointed star had been carved into my hand with some sharp object and that the blood ran rivulets down the side before dripping rapidly to the ground. My first thought upon seeing this was that I had been a fool in thinking my persecutor had changed her nature simply because she had changed her clothes. I must have been unable to satisfy her like Jack and Bill before me, and now she had transformed back into her wild state and was preparing to torture and kill me like she had them. I became immediately frightened and glanced around crazily.

Towards the pool of water by the boulder, I found Lilith. She faced me, completely still. This was not totally unexpected, but she wore an ornate devil mask upon her face which once again prevented me from seeing her true features. The leer it sent me was intended to instill apprehension and fear. I quickly noticed the bowie knife she held down by her waist. It jutted out perpendicularly in my direction.

"What's going on, Lilith?" I asked nervously.

She said nothing in reply. Instead, she took a couple steps toward me. The knife rose to a more menacing position.

"This is stupid," I said. "Quit playing around." I couldn't help but grow more worried. I had hoped that I would be safe after last night, but considering my immediate situation I knew that I had thought wrong. It didn't occur to me that perhaps this was some sort of trial by fire. Images of my friends and their slashed and bleeding bodies returned in quick array.

Lilith moved another step closer and shifted the blade into a military style hold with the pommel facing forward. Then, she paused. She was obviously undergoing some internal struggle, determining whether I should be slain or not. I back up a space, as she thought out her actions in her head, and inadvertently moved myself closer to the nearby drop off. Reacting to my motion, her advance abruptly continued again like the instinct of an animal sensing fear in its prey. She had come to some diabolical resolve, and she speeded up her approach until she was almost pressing the blade lengthwise against my abdomen. I could feel my breath automatically tighten in my lungs so that I wouldn't exhale and be the cause of my own injury. I had nowhere to go. I was trapped.

"I can't believe you are doing this," I blurted out. "What about last night? Did nothing happen between us? Are you going to pretend that it never happened? I fell in love with you last night. Do you want to deny that?"

Anger and frustration and fear radiated out from my body. Whether it was my passionate proclamation of love, or the fury I exuded, that caused her to hesitate again, I couldn't be sure, but whatever the reason it provided me with a window of opportunity to act. My hands snaked out rapidly and gripped her forearms. She cried out in desperation and tried to free herself so that she could slash at me. I held on tenaciously, forcing our struggle to send us into a spinning motion. We circled around each other at a demonic speed until the centrifugal pattern of our whirling split us apart. I fell backward to land in the pool of water, while Lilith flew out over the drop off with a tortured, "noooooo!"

I was on my feet in seconds, racing over to the ledge to learn of her fate. She had fallen about fifty yards down the cliff and crashed onto an outcropping of small rock. It appeared that she had bounced off the cliff face a couple times before landing nearly head first into the stone protrusion where her neck was snapped. It had to be a painful, though hopefully quick, way to die. The mask she wore had also taken a decent amount of damage from the impact, and it was split into three pieces, one of which looked like a large shard. For the first time she had appeared in my life, I could actually see her face. She appeared young and innocent from up here, and if I might say it, at peace with herself. She was absolutely beautiful. The thought of the loss of a beauty like her in the world caused my eyes to mist. She may have been a killer, and have set her sights on me, but she had been truly alive, something few people could state.

I tore my eyes from her broken form and gazed off into the sky. The day was currently cloudless and warm, but over the western mountain peaks I could see a dark build up promising a heavy evening storm. Fortunately, I was once again able to notice smoke from the location of the fire I seen before across the valley. My secret campers had remained in the area it seemed, and they were still unknowingly providing me with a beacon that would guide me out of this wilderness I had so recently become lost in. If I started in that direction right away, I might be able to get there before the rain came.

Staggering away from the deathly spot, I nudged something on the ground. Glancing down, I noticed the bowie knife lying wedged in some dirt. Lilith must have let go of it when she had fallen to her death. For some reason, I bent over to pick it up, though I was not sure why. Some internal voice told me that I needed to hold onto it. It felt warm in my hand, even comfortable, and the smoothness of its metal somehow calmed the pain of the symbol Lilith had etched into my palm. I tested the blade's weight with a few slashes in the air. My strokes moved with effortless precision. It seemed to me that it had been predetermined long ago by some ancient power that I was to be coupled with this blade in the here and now. With new born confidence, I set out in search of my unseen campers, and I knew that from this point on I would be prepared for any attacks from other people. I had the power, I had learned of its source, and my fate would be mine to decide. If I gained one thing from Lilith, it was that I had to take an active part in determining the course of my life. No one would control me evermore.

Darkness fell before I reached the campsite. I could see the flickering light of the fire up ahead between the trees, and back behind me the thundering cloud of the impending storm followed close at my heels. I was sweaty and hungry, and my brain buzzed like the droning of a swarm of bees. I was having trouble thinking clearly. The only thing I could focus on was my grip upon the knife. I had not let go of it since I had left the peak where Lilith's body was left to decay and be reclaimed by the earth, and I held onto it strongly as my sole link to reality. Its pressure managed to keep me conscious. Three figures huddled around the fire ahead of me. Three females by the sound of it, their high pitched voices chatting merrily about everything from boyfriends to sex to clothes to how good the food they had cooked tasted. It sounded so normal and domestic. A broad smile cracked my face at the thought of it. I considered the knife in connection to their simple conversation. I realized that it would probably terrify them to see me appear in their camp with a knife at my side, my features all disheveled and furry. I decided that it would be smarter to hide it for awhile and risk a stroll through the chaos of my disjointed thoughts, sans their physical connection with the real world. I dropped the knife into some unique looking bushes near the clearing where they had set up camp, it was a type of foliage that I could easily locate later, and I kept on walking at a steady pace. I could tell that the women heard me treading across the fallen leaves by this time, because they stopped talking to each other and turned their heads in my direction. The continued thought of my sudden appearance into their tranquil site extended my grin from ear to ear. I must have looked a fright with greasy, wind-blown hair and smudged dirt on my face. I probably looked like Bigfoot or the horned god of Ireland, and the mental image caused me to laugh convulsively on the inside. This was going to be fun. I, of course, held the element of surprise, and I would definitely use it. My smile preceded me into the smoky circle of their camp.

I knew that the knife could wait.

Border Crossing

The moment passes, but its power leaves him rigid, yet mobile, stiffened upright, and electrified with every nerve in his body screaming a high note. His muscles refuse to unwind. He finds himself striding like a wolf by the time he realizes what has happened. At the street corner, he wills his body to pause. With difficult restraint, the young man stands in place hoping to understand the strange sensation that just occurred. His consciousness liquefies, causing all thoughts to trickle rapidly towards his throat, and his usually adroit mental fingers cannot grasp anything to pull into the bright spotlight of focused cognition.

What was that?

His recovering mind, the normally helpful companion to his less than heedful self, replies that it cannot interpret the occurrence. Not enough data it says, throwing out the stimuli in a torrent of information—strange feeling of ennui followed by some sort of deep ignition, or throbbing, perhaps, that seems to have forced a subterranean neural shockwave out across the whole body—as if by presenting these facts, his mind hopes to get him to agree that the collected data is insufficient for determining any results. Where did this shockwave originate from? His mind pleads ignorance. Well, what were the effects of this internal explosion? Nothing that can be quantified, other than an increase in heart rate and an odd feeling of unease or hyperactivity. A frown solidifies upon his face. He feels that he cannot accept these answers. All occurrences have explanations, and all bodily activity can be traced to its source, especially in a case such as this. He must have a way to determine the root of this event.

One potential cause, he reasons, centers around the recent death of his grandfather and the impending funeral he must attend. He had been summoned two days ago from down south and requested to drive immediately up to this rural western town in Wyoming where the wind blows incessantly and the land stretches for miles in every direction. Out to the west, the mountains form a jagged silhouette when the sun sets, but mostly they hide behind heat created haze. It is not hard to imagine this place as the end of the world; the air exudes an atmosphere of desolation and hopelessness. This site will be perfect for a funeral, he concludes. The solemn air will help maintain a serious purity, and the continuous gusts of dirt and isolation will assist the spirit in departing the world.

Goodbye. You may leave. There is nothing here to make you stay; nothing but dust and boredom and walking corpses. Fly away free soul. Your suffering has ended.

A dizzy spell overcomes the young man, and he reaches out to a pole bearing two city street names for support. He leans up against it using his arm as a prop. Where have these thoughts come from? Dust and the walking dead? Since when had he become so morbid? Using his free arm, he wipes imaginary sweat from his face and stares down the cement sidewalk noticing all the little inconsistencies like the hairline crack across one of the sections or the chipped portion on the rounded part of the curb where some heavy object collided and won the battle of solidity. Yes, this is strange. He realizes that he is not feeling like himself just now.

Recent memories flood his brain; the anxiousness of the drive northward dodging frenetic Denver traffic; the bittersweet reunion with family and loved ones; the terrible weight of watching his grandfather slip further into a coma, his skin slipping with him, its pallid consistency hanging taffy-like upon the bones, then that final call, the phone blaring suddenly in the middle of the night, an alarm that cries—it has ended, you no longer must worry, you no longer must dread, the worst has come—and the midnight visit to the hospital with each person treading silently through the dark chill, honoring the situation's need for quiet and reflection, then the body arranged upon the bed appearing casually funereal to which tonight's mourners are allowed a private visitation, toned down, simplistic, more truthful actually, the body appearing Biblical, like Jesus, wearing nothing but an ivory wrap covering the lower half and yet the face, the face still grandfather's as it was in life though dead now, they it is hard to believe, he has seen this face asleep looking no different, except now it is perhaps a bit more gaunt, he cannot be dead, that is just a story they made up to frighten the children, besides he wouldn't allow for this to happen, he had been so commanding and brilliant in life, but still the evidence lies before him, undeniable, with gaping mouth and empty eyes, he peers down that dismal hole, the lips hanging so lax they completely cover the teeth, and he searches for anything, any sign of life that can tell him this was once a human being, this person once had intimidated him, had been the one genius who had actually awed him and been the catalyst spurring him on his quests for knowledge and understanding, but he finds nothing there, nothing except a void sucking dry this hollow body from within, a void that suggests there is no Heaven to escape to, this is the hated truth, we all sink into obscurity, and life is such a pointless endeavor for all we will find is Nothing.

Ergo cogito, ergo sum. The Latin arises from some unknown recess of his mind. Its sudden appearance startles him. "My name is John," he yells inwardly, "John!" The effort to repress the dizziness with a display of self-realization is ineffective. The spinning in fact intensifies, forcing him to grip the street sign hard, forcing him to hold himself up with his other hand braced against his knee as well. After many minutes, the sound of shoes clapping on cement helps him to return, somewhat, to his senses. He pushes himself upright and glances around apprehensively to determine the location of the disturbance. Nothing. Both to the left and to the right. Empty streets lead off to cross other empty streets, and so on, until the vast nothingness of the plains take over.

He is alone.

A desperate need to be somewhere, steals suddenly through his frame. He feels this compulsion pulling at him, striving to move him with magnetic force, and his feet instinctively start heading in a pre-determined direction. He battles the impulse and turns himself around. His motel lodging is behind him. This was supposed to be a quick stroll—a few moments in the air to clear his head and loosen some of the tension caused by the day's events, not an invitation to feel strange and adventurous. Right now, composure and control need to be maintained. He seems to be lacking in his ability to do so. John manages to reach the block his motel is located at and stiff-walks the remaining stretch to his room. He feels a need to shorten his time in the open and cannot help but notice the vague apprehension rising in him from the recent situation he experienced. The hairs literally stand up on the back of his neck as he increases his speed.

Why is he suddenly sweating?

The room key with the oversized plastic number attached to it leaps about in his fingers. It takes too long to pull it from his trousers, so he quickly jams it into the aperture and twists the lock open before dashing into the room and shoving the door shut. From within the security of the interior's darkness, he stares outside between the slit in the window curtains. For some reason, he expects to see the person whose footsteps he heard earlier. His mind imagines a disheveled, drooling maniac with a knife, and he stares nervously at the Dodge Dart parked nearby in the narrow lot as the most likely place for this madman to hide himself. He visualizes the man crouched behind the rear bumper, waiting for him to stroll by. He imagines the man leaping out from the shadows, eager to scratch off another victim, but no tell tale signs emerge to validate his concerns. The area seems abandoned, and as John passes jittery glances back

Jean-Paul Corriveau

and forth across the deserted city block he sees only emptiness, until, for one second, it appears as if a pure white horse flashes into sight on the curb he has just traversed. Just as he starts to focus on the apparition, an itch causes his eye to twitch temporarily. His vision returns quickly, but the horse has disappeared.

John cannot be sure that his current mental state is not causing him to hallucinate. The fact that this is a possibility makes him even more nervous, and with an uneasy heart he slips under the covers of the bed in search of sleep.

His dreams that night are not pleasant. They begin with him standing outside the entranceway to his office building. The structure has grown immense, stretching skyward until it passes out of sight behind a layer of clouds. Nothing matches the awesomeness of its existence, and it towers with colossal imposition over the human insects crawling about on the landscape below. The sight of this edifice fascinates and belittles John as he floats under the engraved marble archway and into the mouth of the building. His movements jerk and contort in unfamiliar patterns. They are beyond his control. Inside, the building exhibits strange shapes and decorations. This really is not the place he is accustomed to working at in reality. For one, there is no boxlike desk manned by the slovenly security guard with the sallow face and the clipped, formal greeting. There is also no row of elevators waiting to whisk people off to their allotted floor. There is simply a vast darkness extending outward and upward, covered by an impenetrable fog that defies the viewer to break through its obfuscation. Oddly enough, the force that controls his unusual movements pushes him forward and into the void. He streaks along for what seems like hours until he eventually reaches the center of this nether-office. Here, he emerges into a large circle of dim light created by a green-brown pillar crowned in flame. An enormous throne of gold sits at the base of the pillar, and upon the throne reposes a creature that is half goat and half man. The monster's skin shines crimson with blood, and at its feet swarm thousands of naked humans, contorting and gyrating in a pit of filth. Certain faces stand out among the crowd. John recognizes the secretary of team two's boss. She greedily gathers up handfuls of filth and shovels the gooey substance into her wide-jawed mouth. To her right, the obnoxious go-getter in the Sales Department pries his tongue between the buttocks of a man who performs the same action upon another. Nearer to the throne, the senior vice-president rubs the filth across her breasts or throws gob of it at those around her. All of their eyes look glazed and emotionless. The creature upon the throne laughs and draws John's attention away from the sickening scene. It beckons for him to join with the rest. John sneers at its attempt to make him one of the many, but the creature simply cackles louder. It leans its ponderous frame forward and breathes in the aroma of greed, apathy, and indolence emitted by

72

the throng, and as John watches the bulk of the creature appears to increase in size. Deep inside, a part of him understands that the thing desires to continue expanding without limit.

John wakes up the next morning in a wet chill.

The day of the funeral feels eternally slow. After the reception, John excuses himself to the family and walks out into the city. He turns down random streets and moves blindly from here to there. No destination matters. He simply needs time to himself; time to get away from the people and face his sadness fully; time to truly remember the man who was his grandfather without the melodramatic and superficial talk of his grandfather's friends, people he had never met previously nor would ever again. He is sick of hearing the same old phrase, "I knew your grandfather, he was such a wonderful, intelligent man," while he stands smiling plastically, shaking the person's hand or giving them a pseudo-hug with a pat on the back. He is especially upset having to hear, "your poem was so lovely and moving. You really should have that published." He doubts that any of them had really been moved by his writing, the non family members that is. If those people were to read his writing in his journal, without the personal death attached to it, they would never really care about what he had to say. The truth of the matter is that his poem was about a person they casually knew, read while they were attending his funeral in a church, and so they felt obligated to say something 'comforting' and 'friendly' to the writer. Not that John believes there is anything wrong with their actions per se. There exists a certain kindness behind their words, but those words from those strangers do not manage to carry the substance or reality that John currently needs. His grandfather's death bears a most certain effect upon his being and reflecting on that event requires an equal amount of sincerity on his part.

His thoughts, though, seem too fragmented and choppy to focus properly on the loss he has experienced. Every time he turns his thoughts inward, towards moments he had with grandfather in the past, his thoughts keep shifting their direction toward something that is associated with that moment but not emotionally involved. He constantly finds himself thinking about the cathedral where the ceremony had been held. The cathedral is one of those grand structures built primarily to impress the pious and heathen alike. Standing four stories high, if one includes the bell tower, it dwarfs the measly buildings that surround it at the center of town. The cathedral stands as a testament to the might of the Catholic Church through the ages, and John momentarily connects the height of its walls with the building in his dream. He quickly dismisses this juxtaposition. The inside of the cathedral contains a vast space between the vaulted ceiling and its gold chandeliers hanging halfway to the ground and the parishioners pews, and the two facing walls on the side each bear five stained glass windows depicting various saints and martyrs. The windows throw prisms of light onto the far ends of the pews, painting those sitting in those spots various hues of the rainbow, while down the center of the hall the ruby carpet advances toward the altar like a river of blood. In his mind's eye, John flows along on the current of this river until reaching the dais, all the while feeling the pressure of the watchful eyes of the funeral's attendants. The surroundings press in on him. John cannot escape the ambience of the place, and the environment fills him with an unusual energy. He wonders if the others at the funeral feel this too. He wonders if it is actually the presence of God. John sends out mental probes around the building, searching for any entity present, but he detects no life in the slick stone walls. He thinks to himself, "no, the energy in this place comes from those who perceive the structure and accept its sense of mystery, not from some external, inhabiting force."

A nearby sound draws John out of his reverie. Nothing presents itself as the cause of the disturbance, and as he glances around he realizes that he has been wandering the town for quite some time. He has entered an unknown section of the city, and night has fallen, shadowing the sky and the town's surroundings. Amazingly, no weekend traffic or activity intrude upon the area, even though the time must be no later than seven p.m. Nervousness from this ghost town scenario rises in his throat. He rapidly strolls to a street corner in the hopes that one of the city street signs will provide him with some indication of his location, but the corner he reaches lacks the desired marker. Moving further down the sidewalk, he increases his pace to a jog, but he finds that the next corner is missing its sign as well. Suddenly, something inside his head guides him down the right hand avenue, and without attempting to question this emerging instinct, he half strolls, half jogs, in that direction praying that his intuition will lead him towards geographic salvation or human assistance. As he moves, he notices a blur of white out of the corner of his eye. Its appearance intensifies the panic now balling up in his abdomen, and his fear grows stronger as he turns this way and that in an attempt to determine the source of the white shadows that appear in his peripheral vision and then disappear when he tries to look directly at them.

John breaks into a run.

As before, the next intersection appears identical to the previous ones, four brick buildings on each side, no street signs or markers, and no indication of life. Fortunately, his internal compass still functions, and it informs him that he should turn left. Without hesitation, he does so. At the next intersection, his internal guide specifies that he should he move down into the earth. John glances around confused. These are level streets. There are no hills, no grades. The directions do not make any sense.

Out of nowhere, the pale white horse from the evening before rears up before him. Fires blaze from its nostrils, and its forelegs strike the air as it snorts in anger at John's presence. John backs away from the beast. He suppresses the instinct to run, despite his reactive fear, and in doing so manages to discover the destination that his instincts had led him to.

Across the street, hangs a large purple, neon sign reading the odd slogan "U Roar Vice" with a flashing arrow pointing down at a darkened staircase running parallel to that building's brick wall. The sign shines bright behind the stallion like the star followed by the wise men in Biblical times, a blunt omen, and John realizes that he must find a way to descend the staircase. Of course, it is obvious that the raging horse has every intention of stopping him from accomplishing that goal, though he cannot understand why that should be.

Putting his competitive sports skills into play, John performs a quick feint to the right. The horse moves in that direction, and immediately John bolts back to the left. The horse naturally completes the first step, but it is slow in reacting to his reversal. The outcome is that John manages to dodge the horse's initial and only block. Exploiting this opening, John rushes with the speed of a pro running back to the metal railing on one side of the staircase, and upon arriving spins about in case of an attack from behind by the horse. Unexpectedly, the stallion maintains its position in the center of the intersection. Then it begins stomping one hoof repeatedly and snorting in vexation at having been eluded. It cocks its head to stare at him with almost human directness. This unnerves John greatly, and he screams, "What do you want?" The horse remains silent for a few seconds, glaring at him, before abruptly trotting off into the gathering fog. John gazes at the disappearing figure, mystified, and shakes his head.

What on earth is going on here?

The stairs descend into a densely packed gloom, and John feels unsure about descending. At the base, he can see the faint outline of a door set into the brick of the left hand wall. Tiny flickers of candlelight escape out from a gap at the bottom. "Faery fire," he tells himself. "If I walk down there and no door really exists, then I will be at the mercy of whatever evil lurks in the darkness." After a few seconds of debate, he decides to proceed, albeit with reservations. Tentatively, John moves downward step by step. He maintains a hold on the angled metal hand rail, but nothing impedes his progress or jumps out to attack him. After a lengthy period of time, he reaches the bottom and ascertains that the glow does indeed emanate from behind a badly chipped wooden door. John grips the cool doorknob and tugs gently, tensing for the expected shriek of rusty hinges, but the door swings open with a silent whisper.

A concrete tunnel leads off into shadowy murkiness from behind the entrance. Candles have been ensconced in jagged holes located sporadically along its length, and they flickered from the rush of air created by the opening door. Water trickles down the sides of the passage to form shallow pools in the low areas of the floor, and an odor of age and earthiness pervades the area. About twenty feet away, the tunnel veers left, and a brighter glow, along with the sound of strange electronic music wrap around the corner. John decides that he has stumbled upon some vagabond's hidden lair. "Have I been led here to obtain mystic advice from some urban guru? Am I to gain knowledge of how to sort out the mental trauma surrounding my grandfather's death?" As he speculates these questions, his excitement over the possibility of wisdom gained overshadows his subconscious apprehension, and he moves along down the passageway.

The corner leads into a small basement room lit by two gigantic candelabra. The ancient brass fixtures each bear twenty fat candles, and each candle's flame appears to be the size of one's thumbs. The candelabra sit upon a short square table covered by a white silk cloth. A blue robed man, his head covered by a cowl, relaxes behind the table on a beat up Papazzan chair. To his right, stands a younger man in a black t-shirt and jeans. As John enters the room, the younger man whips out a nasty looking bowie knife from a sheath upon his belt and yells, "what the fuck are you doing here? Are you looking for pain?"

John stops cold, unsure of what to do.

The fair-skinned young man slides closer while holding the knife out at arm's length menacingly. "I said, are you looking for pain," he repeats, "because if you are then we are the ones to give it to you!" The young man stops to wait for John's reply, but John simply returns his stare and holds his ground. This surprises the young man, who analyzes John's stance and then abruptly drops his arm and plops down on a worn sofa. He begins to scrape underneath his fingernails with the point of the blade. "Shit," he cusses. "He's just another fucking dead man and not worth the bother. Leave dead man! We don't want you here."

The blue robed man sits up at this point and addresses the young man in a stern, paternal tone. "Do you think that the dead don't despise those who live? If he truly were a dead man, than we could be in serious danger. But he found us here, you overlook that, and it means that he has potential. Our kind are too few. He may join us."

The young man hangs his head in angry embarrassment and does not reply to the criticism. The established hierarchy is readily apparent.

The blue robed man then turns toward John to apologize. "I am sorry for his rude behavior, but he is at a stage that is quite vocal and uninhibited. Please, come in…" and his hesitation lets John know that he should introduce himself. John has no trouble answering.

"My name is John."

"Nice to meet you, John. Welcome to my abode. Do sit down and relax." The man gestures to a couch on his left.

John scans the room as he sits. Deep shadows cover the walls, and their presence conceals the true dimensions of the place giving it the appearance of limitless depth. Few accoutrements adorn the room other than the furniture. There is a small stereo and case, a CD rack, and a bookshelf stacked with thick worn novels. Incense has been wedged between two of the books on the shelf, and it burns slowly, filling the room with a musky, ancient odor. Also, Christmas lights hang down from the darkness of the ceiling. The effect of their fuzzy, colored lights is like a sedative. John begins to feel light-headed, and he leans back into the sofa and allows the tension in his mind to loosen. It is a pleasurable sensation to bask in. Because of this, it takes a few moments for him to notice that the young man stands before him with his arm stuck out, this time in mockery of a formal greeting.

"Hi, my name is Geryon. Pleased to meetchaa!"

John grips the young man's hand and replies, "you too," while receiving a slightly over enthusiastic handshake. "That's a unique name you have, Geryon. What is its ethnicity?"

Geryon gives John an odd glance as he returns to his own sofa and laughs. John becomes perplexed.

"Don't mind him," the blue robed man intrudes. "He thinks he is being funny."

"It's not funny! It fits!"

"Yes, but it is also limiting."

"John listens to their banter and remains in confusion over their wordplay. He decides to keep silent.

"Shall I tell you his Christian name?" the blue robed man asks, though his question is actually a quip aimed at Geryon. The other youth casts a spiteful glance at him. The two stare menacingly and playfully at each other until Geryon asks, "Don't you mean Jewish name?" Both men break out in boisterous laughter. The enigmatic joke passes over John's head and reinforces his resolve to remain quiet. Fortunately, the blue robed man in his capacity as host does not take long to resolve the issue for him.

"His real is David, like the mighty king of yore. I would tell you my name, too, but unfortunately it has been long forgotten through the sands of time. I have been so many things over the years that I can no longer differentiate between this identity and that."

"Yes, now he is just the Master," jests Geryon as he pronounces the word 'master' in imitation of dubbed voice actors in seventies Kung-Fu movies.

John feels uneasy listening to their casual dueling over names and titles. All his old, Catholic teachings about Satan during Sunday catechism, and how Satan is called Legion due to his numerous appellations, return to him, and he finds himself recalling his dream from the previous night again. True, the blue robed man does not bear resemblance to the creature in his dream, and the room, though dark, does not have the permeation of evil that the other orgiastic domain had, but there lingers an undeniable expression of the unnatural about everything here.

"Are you the devil?" he inquires.

His words elicit a hearty laugh from the blue robed man who states, "No, I was a devil once, but now I am a magician. Geryon, here, is our resident devil these days."

"That' correct," Geryon suddenly screams and starts pouncing on the sofa. "Fuck my bones!" To John's astonishment, the young man begins dry humping one of the cushions.

"All right," the blue robed man interrupts Geryon's festivities. "I believe everyone should turn it down a notch."

With an extravagant flourish, the blue robed man whisks a foot long, opaque purple plastic cylinder out from under the papazzan chair. He sets it in front on himself, perpendicular to the floor, and proceeds to fill the metal bowl sprouting from its side with a dry plant-like substance that he had stashed in one of his robe's side pockets. As John watches, he picks the tube up with one hand, places the open top end of the cylinder to his mouth, and lights the leafy substance with a Bic lighter. Smoke fills the inside of the cylinder, and the man rapidly inhales to draw it into his mouth.

Is that marijuana? John asks.

"Why, yes it is," Geryon nods humorously. He has resumed his seat and leans forward towards the blue robed man, rubbing his together with an eager expression that borders on the maniacal. John's nervousness creeps up once more to grasp at the back of his skull, and he wonders if he should attempt to depart the area and avoid an uncomfortable situation with these strange men and drugs and all. Neither of the men notices John's distress. The blue robed man simply passes the cylinder and lighter over to Geryon who accepts them gratefully before re-enacting the ritual just performed by his friend. As Geryon begins to inhale, the blue robed man in counter-point exhales a massive cloud into the air that quickly billows through the room and infuses it with a pungent sweet odor. The smoke leaves wispy trails above their heads that resemble spirits flying through the skies. Something about the motions of the smoke and the scent help John to relax again. He decides against leaving for the moment.

Across the room, Geryon sucks up as much smoke as his lungs will hold, taking a couple minutes to drag off the tube, then he stands and stretches over the table to hand the cylinder to John. His body jerks violently as he performs this action. John sees that Geryon is trying to hold the smoke in for as long as possible, and a strange noise, like the combined sound of a snort and a cat sneezing, erupts from his throat. John hesitantly grabs the proffered objects and pulls them to his lap. He attempts to replay his host's actions in his mind, believing that will help him to utilize the device without something going awry or him appearing foolish. Fortunately, a question posited by the blue robed man provides him with a temporary reprieve from his trial by fire.

"So, John, what type of guy are you? What do you do?"

"I work for a company in Denver. I'm just up here for a couple days attending my grandfather's funeral. I'll be heading home tomorrow to get back to work."

"A company man. How...nice. I am sorry to hear about your grandfather, though. Were you very close to him?"

John glances down at his feet as he replies. "Well, yes and no. I mean, I loved him and all, but we never really talked. I guess you could say he was more of an inspiration to me. I always looked up to him like some kind of...oh I don't know. He was amazingly intelligent, and I suppose I always wanted to achieve this state of omniscience that he seems to have attained."

The blue robed man passed Geryon a knowing glance and intoned, "omniscience, hmmm. That is very interesting. I would say that you had quite a connection with the man. These must be difficult times for you. I can't imagine why you would want to return to work so soon."

Oh, I don't, but the company only provides a couple of days leave for a death in the family. We can't go over our quota, or we will be written up. I can't risk losing my position."

"That's not very sensitive of them. Nor humanistic as well."

"I know. But my case isn't so bad. Not like Jenny's situation a couple months ago. She was this girl in our department who was pregnant, and when the time came for her to give birth, the company told her they wouldn't cover her maternity leave because she had missed the hiring deadline for coverage by one week."

The blue robed man's lips curled up. "Do you think that's acceptable for them to do?"

"Well, no, but the company states that they put regulations in place to keep everything running smoothly and to prevent abuse."

"I don't agree with that line of thought," the blue robed man states, "or with your complaisance."

"I'm sorry, but I just don't know what I can do about it."

The blue robed man stares intently at John. For a few moments, he appears as if he is going to start yelling, but then he calms down and cracks a smile. "Just smoke up, my boy. I'll fill you in on how to proceed."

John does not feel consoled by the abrupt change in the blue robed man's attitude, but he carefully puts the cylinder up to his mouth anyway. He has a difficult time handling both the cylinder and the lighter at the same time, and he fumbles to ignite the lighter. Once lit, though, he holds the flame to the leafy substance in the bowl, watches it crackle and turn orange, and then begins to suck hard inside the tube. Unlike the other two men, the results of his actions are lackluster. Hardly any smoke is produced within the cylinder. The water in the tube bubbles loudly, yet nothing happens otherwise. He inhales deeper, thinking that he is not creating enough of a suction to pull in the smoke, but this simply causes him to turn red in the face. Geryon and the blue robed man laugh hysterically and roll around on the furniture.

"You gotta cover the carb," Geryon points out, "the little hole on the other side of the bowl."

John's face turns a brighter shade of red from embarrassment. He searches all over the tube for the hole and finally finds it conveniently located near where his thumb was holding the cylinder. Placing his thumb on the hole, and then re-enacting the previous steps John is successful this time in manipulating the device. Warm smoke pours into his lungs, feeling like the exploration of wiggling fingers tickling him internally, and he unceremoniously coughs out the smoke within a matter of seconds.

"Try again," the blue robed man suggests gently, "you will get it."

John repeats the process, and this time the smoke settles smoothly inside his lungs like a velvet snowfall. He mentally focuses on the sensation and then hands the cylinder back to the blue robed man who immediately re-packs the bowl with more pot. Shortly thereafter, John blows out the smoke he has been holding in, and watches it pour out in a tumultuous amount from his lips. He feels his body begin to relax, and he sinks back into the soft, warm embrace of the couch's cushions.

The procedure of inhale, pass, and refill gets repeated two more times by the trio, so that by the time the blue robed man finally shoves the cylinder back under his papazzan chair John's head is spinning slightly and has a rather airy quality to it.

For some reason, John notices the music again, now, despite the fact that it has been playing since he first arrived. It rolls out a continuous rhythm with electronic and real drums thumping out furious pagan beats that cause his blood to pulsate faster. The percussion in the music is backed by harmonic synthesizers and keyboards which flutter, rise, and dip like falcons on the wind. There are also various samples of voice and noises, ethereal sounds, that seek to lift him out of his chair. He notices how his mind levitates up out of his body, and he feels freer than ever before in his life. The body is simply a package, he thinks, a hindrance to a mind that wants to roam wildly through the celestial ether.

The music calls for his mind to follow.

John associates it with the expurgated tale of the Pied Piper from children's storybooks, not the original Hamlin legend. The piper played entrancing lilts upon his flute and drew the rats from the villages of his homeland to cleanse them. Except, perhaps, from another perspective it could be argued that the piper was not interested in saving the towns so much as helping return the rats to the natural tranquility of the countryside. The revelation of a second possible reading shocks John. "Had the piper sought to remove the rats from the evils of the social world," he wonders, "and assisted them in regaining access to their primordial roots?" Were the rats perhaps the victims instead of a scourge?" A smile broadens across his face. No sooner does he begin to enjoy this alternative he had created when another twist to the concept crosses his mind. In this area of the nation circulates the native tale of Kokopele. Kokopele, like the Pied Piper, was a musician who wandered from tribe to tribe. He walked across the world, naked to the elements, and he played his instrument to summon women out from their teepees and make love to them. Again, there exists a theme centering on a mystical, mysterious being that, drawing people out, acts as a leader and directs people toward a forgotten state of inhibition and liberty. It surprises John that he has not noticed the similarity between the two tales prior to now. It is so simple a connection.

The music shifts to a guitar based groove, and John looks up to see Geryon at the stereo feeding it more CD's. The blue robed man has pulled out his own bowie knife, an older more worn, yet more ornate, version of the one that Geryon had unsheathed earlier, and he sits stroking the dragon headed pommel, replete with bulging eyes and sharp fangs. John glances about for something to interact with himself and locates a notebook and pen upon the tabletop. He languidly grabs these items and begins writing down the thought flowing unrestrictedly from his mind. He writes…

White heart in the wilderness
Behold the innocence of the deer
Not noticeable through the foliage
Of the people easily swayed by the wind.

You are beauty personified
Graceful in your simplicity
As you slip from tree to tree
Your nature covered by all the color.

What is it that makes me
Want to see you die
And fall blood red
A thorn in your side.

I love you!

"What are you writing?"

John raises his eyes up from the paper to find the blue robed man staring at him intently.

"Oh, just a poem," he replies, feeling flustered for some reason. He tries to inconspicuously fold up the sheet he was writing on and stuff it in his pocket. The blue robed man stops him.

"You're a poet? Excellent. Please, read us your poem."

"No, I'm not really a poet," John stipulates. "I just write things from time to time."

"That's not true, my boy. We are all poets and artists of various forms here. You wouldn't have reached this place if you weren't."

"Yeah, man," Geryon adds. "Like me. I'm a poet of life. I fuck things to death. Woo hoo."

Geryon leaps off the sofa and starts performing ludicrous pelvic thrusts similar to the players from the Rocky Horror Picture Show. The three of them cannot help but laugh out loud, and the release soothes John enough that he is willing to read his poem. When he finishes, the other two nod their heads like they are agreeing with an argument he made.

The blue robed man is the first to speak. "That was very good. Care to explain it to us?"

"Well," John considers, "I'm not sure what it means, but I think that it has to do with my interest in weird people and why they are different from 'normal' people. They are the deer, the weird people that is, and for some reason I feel like I need to save them and bring them back to the norm, but to do that I have to kill them."

"That's interesting, John," the blue robed man says, "but I think you are overlooking something...or maybe lying to yourself. I think, first, that you don't want to bring the deer back to the norm exactly. You find the deer beautiful in its whiteness. All the colored trees, or normal people, are filled with pointless distractions, the color, and are easily swayed by public opinion. Your words make that state of being seem contemptible, and you wouldn't want that for the deer. No, you simply aren't for the norm. What you want is to actually help the deer out of the weakness that its innocence breeds. You want to help it to ascend to the next stage in life, a stronger stage. Does that make sense? Good. Secondly, I think that you yourself are the deer. It's really yourself that you want to help strengthen. You want to kill some unacceptable aspect of your current lifestyle.

John purses his lips and half-heartedly nods. He is not eager to accept what the blue robed man is saying, but he cannot help but believe that the interpretation is the correct one. He sees how the passages follow along those lines, and he wonders if perhaps his subconscious is speaking through his writing without him realizing it.

"How about I recite a piece I composed yesterday?" the blue robed man continues. "It's a little something I call...well, who cares what I name it?"

The man pauses a moment for effect and then dives into his poem with gusto.

"The wrecks of civilization surround me.
I don't speak of crumbling temples, broken pottery,
Or cobwebbed libraries.

I speak of living decay,
Of people without souls,
Of architecture without purpose,
And education without learning.
Our society is dead and does not realize.

Most eyes I meet are glazed.
Most actions mechanical.
Words today are written by monkeys.

It is time for us to burn the rot.
Let us start fresh once more
And rebuild the world with a stronger metal.
Perhaps then we will find meaning."

"Bravo," Geryon clamors as the blue robed man finishes, "fucking beautiful," and proceeds to clap outrageously from his perch on the sofa.

John looks over at his lunatic companion and blinks his eyes. Could he be seeing things? Is the drug causing him to hallucinate? He swears that a naked, raven haired woman lies on the sofa in front of Geryon masturbating. He rubs his eyes and looks again. She remains in place, manipulating her clitoris with deft precision. Oddly enough, Geryon seems unaware of her presence. John turns to the blue robed man for confirmation of her existence and finds an elderly naked man standing directly behind his other companion. The naked man hold both his hands on either side of the blue robed man's head, and a soft golden glow emanates from between his fingers to create a halo effect around the cowl. Both of these silent, nude figures seem to have materialized from nowhere.

"What is the matter?" the blue robed man asks querulously.

"I think I'm seeing things. There is a naked man and woman in the room."

"You see Vani and Vic?" Geryon sputters. "Oh man! You were right, dude. He is one of us."

Geryon's words are incomprehensible to John. He glances back and forth from Geryon to the blue robed man for assistance. They, in turn, stare at each incredulously. The blue robed man speaks first.

"This is a surprising development. We had not thought you to be so far along. What you are seeing are manifestations of our innermost selves. These beings personify, ne embody, the driving forces behind our lives. They are not real in the corporeal sense, but their energy has great influence upon our existence. The fact that you can already see them means that you have advanced to the first state of being. I believe congratulations are in order. We should celebrate.

Both Geryon and the blue robed man stand up suddenly. Geryon turns off the CD player, and the blue robed man removes his robe to reveal a frilly, white pirate-styled shirt and leather pants beneath. He appears much younger than John had imagined him to be beneath the cowl. As he drops the robe onto the sofa, John notices his left hand moving strangely and realizes that it is actually a prosthetic limb. John looks away quickly to keep the blue robed man from noticing the shock cross his face. Glancing at the exit, he sees a painting that went overlooked when he had entered the underground chamber. Lifting himself up, he walks over to analyze it. The effort his body requires for this normally simple action amazes him until he remembers that he had actually become stoned on forty-five minutes before.

The painting turns out to be one of those surreal works, utilizing abstract metaphysics, a style made popular earlier in the century and now reclaimed by the Mtv generation at the end of the century. The scene is set in space with specks of stars dotting the entire skyscape. Three masks float in this aether: the right one a humorous, white-faced clown with a hint of a sinister side in its smile, the middle one a handsome fifties gentleman complete with smoking pipe and respectable slick hair style, the left one a fiendish demon with green pus covered skin, red cat eyes, and vicious fangs. The left and right masks look inward to the middle mask as well as at each other. The middle one stares straight out of the picture at the viewer. A beam of white shoots up the center of the picture, engulfing the middle mask, and it is difficult to distinguish whether the beam is simple shaft of light or some type of container. In the lower right corner, the painting is signed "Killer".

The no longer blue robed man appears behind John and slaps him on the backs. "Like my friend's painting?" he asks. The words seem to circle slowly around John's head before swirling into his ears. "It has quite a lot of meaning. Why don't you dwell on the point of it, and when you think you have figured it out we can discuss." John feels unable to reply. His mouth refuses to open, and his dry tongue seems to weigh a hundred pounds. He finds himself being led out of the room, escorted down the dank hallway, and back out into the city. His feet do not so much move as float on the air like Hermes. As he glides along, he wonders what the painting is trying to convey. Is it saying that masks are the primary aspect of existence? But why are there three of them? Is that how the artist views the Holy Trinity? Or are they supposed to be the Anti- Trinity? John finds no ground for establishing a base to answer any of these questions. To make things more complicated, the masks each stare in a different direction. Why? One would think that they would all face the same way, in the same direction or out at the viewer. There seems to be no sensible reason why the artist painted what he or she did, and John wraps himself up so deeply in his analysis that he hardly notices the journey made by the three of them. By the time his vision returns to the outside world, he finds that they have entered an ill lit tavern and are sitting down in a booth toward the back of the room.

The realization that they have trekked through the streets of town alters his pattern of thought. It dawns on him to ask his now gothic looking friend about his earlier interaction with the ghostly stallion at the intersection by the stairwell.

"Um," he mumbles, almost incoherently. "I was wondering if you knew anything about a white horse roaming the streets. Right before I met you guys, I bumped into one, and it tried to attack me. I swear it was deliberately trying to keep me from finding the stairwell that led to your basement abode."

The no longer blue robed man nods. "So you've met the Beast, and, by the sounds of it, defeated it, at least temporarily. I guessed as much when I saw you enter the room. That is good. It means you are well on your way to joining us. Now, what we must do is prepare you to ride the beast, for only then will you be able to raise yourself up to the next highest state of being."

John recalls his fear concerning the horse, and it causes him to react negatively to his companion's assumptions. "I don't understand. What are you talking about? Why are you saying that I am supposed to become like you? Is that why all this strange stuff is happening? And what type of place is this?"

The questions explode from John's lips as he glances around the establishment. It is obviously not the typical drinking hole. Black paint splashed with phosphorescent green, red, and yellow indiscriminately coats the walls. The patrons slide about in a variety of leather and lace outfits, all of them slinky and seductive, like the rock and roll poster children of Lucifer, and their uninhibited sexuality hangs in the air like a thick musk. In his mind, John momentarily considers them to be punks and freaks, but then he realizes that those are the words his co-workers at the company would use. The frequency with which he is battered by their prejudiced outbursts has started to infect his mind. The mainstream group uses guilt, financial pressure, and mass domination, either directly or indirectly, to force him and other free-thinkers and innovators to reject their autonomy and conform. The thought flashes like a supernova in his brain. It is a major epiphany brought on by the marijuana and his writing. He declares to himself, "I do not agree with the values of the system in which I live. It is an existence built on anger and subservience and intolerance." John rolls the words over and over again in his head and thinks that this must be what the no longer blue robed man meant by saying that John was one of them. He…they…probably others…are the strange ones in his poem. They walk through the woods in a white and pure state of being, and they ignore the driving wind that blows the trees about them. The realization hits bittersweet.

Geryon suddenly distracts his thoughts by plopping down into the booth with a loud clink of beer bottles. He slides one over to the no longer blue robed man and one over to John. The no longer blue robed man, who John has playfully started imagining to be a High Priest of Harmful Matter (like the Californian rock star labeled by a sex-deprived appellate judge), takes a deep swig, slumps comfortably against the hard wood backing of the booth, and assumes a professorial air.

"Desire," he preaches, "when stifled may become a very dangerous emotion. Similarly, Being when stifled can become a very maddening experience. Environment plays a role in releasing both, but problems arise when negative environments cannot be escaped. A person is forced to endure something that should not be. Then, the solution might lie via an outlet. For the majority of sheep society, this occurs in the traditional trek to the local watering hole where a non-controversial, non-threatening, yea non-cognitive release takes place. Others need more than this simple expedient."

He swivels in his seat to stare at John, but before he can speak Geryon slams down his bottle and raises a finger to counter the Priest's words.

"No, dude! There is nothing wrong with heading to the clubs to try to pick up a little tail. Hell, we have our clubs and the dead men have their sports bars. Why fuck up our well established segregation?"

The Priest ignores Geryon, but replies to him nonetheless as he addresses John. "Unfortunately, Geryon's anger towards the discriminating population in our society causes him to discriminate as badly as those he vilifies. He still has to learn to detest the action, or the system, and not the man or woman." Geryon shakes his head disgustedly, empties about half a bottle, pops something he had kept in a plastic pouch into his mouth and lurches off to the dance floor in search of less disagreeable companionship. The Priest does not seemed surprised by this reaction and continues his tutelage with John, who has started to regain cohesive thought and a more linear stream of consciousness since getting high. "Many people find it hard to believe that Geryon once was, and still is, a very sensitive person. But that is the nature of the stage he inhabits—to be brash and bold and overly self-confident and expressive. C'est la vie! At least now, I can talk to you without any interference. What I have been attempting to convey in my nonsequitur manner of speaking is that there are quite a few different states of consciousness or realities that exist in life. The reason you found us is because you are starting to become aware of these alternate dimensions and are opening up to the innumerable possibilities available to humankind. Something in life has gotten you to start questioning the repressive nature of our capitalistic American culture."

"My grandfather's death," John blurts excitedly. "That is what has me thinking so strangely."

The Priest seems a little astonished by the outburst, but like Geryon's rudeness a moment ago he takes it in and smoothly continues with his explanation. "Perhaps so, but the important thing to focus on is the present. You need answers and explanations. In this department, you are fortunate to have me here. Many of our kind have had to obtain knowledge of ourselves through extensive searching and introspection. You are being given the guided tour. What we are, put simply, are Outsiders. We are the people who walk the byways of the universe hoping to find ourselves and help humankind evolve into a higher state of freedom and understanding. Let me state it in a more poetic manner. It is easier for me that way."

"There is a path that must be trod alone.
Few dare traverse it,
and even fewer have the stamina to continue along it.
It is the road between,
the night corridor to purist light.
And as you walk, all horror manifests.
And if you finish, all suffering enters into you.
But then you have reached the center that is all."

He pauses to let his words settle. John sits beside him unable to speak while out on the dance floor, Geryon grinds his hips against some dark haired dominatrix who appears much too shy for her attire. Inaudible invocations of love fall from his lips in conjunction with the laser light in an attempt to weave a spell upon her. That is when John notices the glint of Geryon's bowie knife from under his shirt where it has been stuffed behind the beltline and wonders why Geryon brought it with him.

The Priest shakes his head.

"She will be the fifth one this week. He is quite insatiable, that boy. But she seems to be his favorite. He might fall in love with her, I think, and that is a dangerous game for him to play." John starts to ask what is meant by this, but the Priest resumes his discourse before the young man can utter a syllable. "You see, John, Geryon is walking the path to enlightenment right now…as I am. But I have the good fortune of being farther along, having tread it for a greater breadth of time. He still needs to learn what I am about to tell you. It is something that you must always keep in mind as you walk the path yourself. It is simply this. If one searches for a specific answer, one can find it with little effort. One can in fact find many answers. The point is that one must not stop searching for answers because that is when the repressive systems, such as the one you are now seeking to abandon, arise. There are an infinite number of doors in the universe, and truths are located behind every one of them. Following a single avenue of knowledge eventually leads to madness, destruction, or totalitarianism. The key to existence lies in constant movement, particularly within purity of action. By purity of action, I mean any natural action untainted by the intimidating hand of any system or society. As Outsiders, we embody the understanding that one must strive for continual divergence in order to reach a state of uninfluenced, unmotivated Self. Reaching this state is of course nearly impossible, but it must be attempted. Through discipline and focus, one may come quite near this state of…let me say for lack of a better term…tabla rosa. Does that make sense?"

No, John thinks, but he is afraid to admit his lack of comprehension. He gravely nods at the Priest, who smirks doubtfully.

"Believe me," he says, "this will definitely make sense later on. For now, let me counsel you in the ten proposals I have devised for our kind. They are as follows. One, excess in moderation is the key to life. Two, deny nothing about your nature. Three, repress your desires only in specific and necessary instances. Four, love true friends and family one hundred percent and be unconcerned but kind for all others, unless they cause you harm at which time you may react as you see fit. Five, travel regularly and learn the customs of the places you visit. Six, try everything at least twice with an objective mindset. Seven, regularly practice mind and body synthesis. Eight, fuse with nature whenever possible. Nine, do not do as others say, but rather act as others should act, and ten, expect the unexpected."

"I suppose that I should add that there is one true sacred element in life, and that is children. No adversity or harm should ever befall a child by one's hand despite the proposals I have just stated. Of course, except for this last bit, these guidelines aren't set in stone. One may amend all or any part of these as time passes, and one desires, but these current ideals should form a good place to begin."

"The reason I tell you this is because you should be adaptable to growth and not prone to falling in a rut. That is one of the greatest traps you will face along the path, and it is one that may most warp you in your quest for the divine. Most people improperly experience the divine, if they experience it at all. Now, what I mean by the divine is that state of transcendence by which a person becomes locked into the energies that ebb and flow through all existence. The divine is that root of chaos, that state of fluctuation, underpinning and originating the variants we experience in this universe. The most direct routes to the divine, and the easiest with which to fall into a rut, are through drugs and sex. Each orgasm a person has, each high, shifts that person out of the typical organic and existential state into a vibratory, energetic state. Experience moves from the exterior realm into the interior, where the divine resides. These two states may be fine in the beginning of divinatory exploration, which is why I tell this to you, but unfortunately many come to believe this to be the whole of the process. These two routes become a crutch for the majority who use them to maintain one's position in the divine, while simultaneously enabling an addiction (at which point the experience becomes routine and mundane so that ever more intense and drastic crossovers are required to transition). These people become dependent and hooked upon this corporeal bathing in the divine that they eventually burn out, similar to when a person stares at the sun, even if just for a few seconds, on a regular basis. After so many times, the person goes blind. The cause for this problem of repetition can be found in a couple of facts. One, people forget they are mortal beings in their current state, and two, sex and drugs provide but transient connections with the divine. What people need to do to avoid this common trap along the path is to connect with the divine but not be subsumed by it. In order to accomplish this necessity, one must remove themselves totally from the world of appearance and from all social illusions."

"Whoa there, doc," John interrupts, "you are moving way too fast for me. Besides, how can you know for sure that I am even going to agree to walk on your path anyhow? Tomorrow, I return to my job, and chances are that I will have forgotten this whole interlude by next week."

Jean-Paul Corriveau

The Priest nods his head and smiles. "I am sorry, John," he says, "but I have a tendency to become passionate about this subject when discussing it. After all it is the root of my existence. And you are correct. I have no positive knowledge that you will walk the winding way, though I do know you will never walk MY path. Yet, I can see you have been touched. What I see in your eyes gives me faith. You will do what is needed. How about I explain things in a manner that your mind should readily grasp? Are you familiar with Native American mythology?"

"Not much, no."

"Okay. Well, if you read many of their old tales, particularly those of the Ojib-wa, Ottowa, or other Iroquois tribes you will find that all their stories deal with characters who live outside any village. These individuals are held in high regard because they actively seek ways to learn more about this world, as well as that of the spirit world, and in this strive to improve their state of being. The journeys they undertake to accomplish these goals are often arduous and dangerous. In order to survive these quests, they strengthen their connection with nature, with the land itself, or with their guardian animal spirits, and often they would gain assistance from other powerful spirits, the Manitoes, who are men endowed with great magical abilities. The Natives tell these tales about these spiritual warriors because they want their people to realize that the ultimate goal in one's life is to find one's place in the universe and maintain the cosmic balance of nature in the process. Today, we as Outsiders agree with this belief. I could discuss similar positions held in a large variety of mythologies from other cultures to support this stance on life. Take for example, the tales of Jason and the Argonauts and King Ulysses from Greek mythology, Sinbad, from Persian mythology, Gautama from Buddhist religion, Loki, Thor, and Odin in Norse mythology. Even Jesus spent his days travelling about Northeastern Africa and the Middle East in the name of Jehovah. I could go on, and with great detail about this subject, but I will spare you that as you seem to want concise arguments. Suffice to say, we as Outsiders have come to hold movement, action, and creativity in the highest esteem based on the lessons of the past."

The Priest halts his exposition, and John cannot help but think he should call him the Shaman now due to the recent turn in the discussion. The Shaman gazes out to the dance floor again where Geryon has turned the center into a veritable display of eroticism. The young man encircles his partner from behind like a serpent; his right hand cupping her half covered breast, from the style of her black leather bodice, while his tongue flicks teasingly against her cheek. The two contort and convulse and appear so wrapped up in their sensuality that they notice nothing about them. They

92

gyrate and kiss and grapple under the colorful lights of the dance floor until their passion rises beyond normal intensity. At that point, the girl grabs Geryon by the back of the neck and stalks off the floor like a Lupe Garou with him in tow.

The Shaman grins and tosses a sly question towards John. "You find that exciting don't you, to have lovers seduce you in public? Wouldn't you like to feel the power of total release? You are only one step away from it on the path, you know."

The Shaman takes a moment to take a swig of beer and then resumes talking. Geryon wrote about his position on the path last week, you know. He scribbled the following parable."

I once went to the President of the United States. He told me, 'read my lips! We need to strengthen this country and save it from the encroachment of non-capitalistic third world parties. Become one of my points of light and spread the righteousness f democracy.' This sound correct to me; I had been raised in accordance with these views. Then I met a Mr. Arafat conferring with an Apache chieftain. Their voices were machine gun fire and the fierce cry of battle. They shouted, 'hear our indignation! We must ignite the world and burn out the forces that oppose us. These oppressive governments are evil and must be destroyed.' I felt the power in their words. I recognized their suffering and knew it was unjust. But God floated down to me. He had the Holy Scriptures tattooed across the palms of his hands, and he spoke in a whisper that caused the earth to quake. 'My son, you know you are a child of mine and that I hold the ultimate power in the universe. Ignore these others because they do not care for the well being of your soul. Belief in my laws is mandatory for eternal bliss.' Soon after, I encountered Buddha seated in the shade of a giant cobra. He was quiet for some time, but finally, spoke. 'You may listen to others without impudence for their words are like wind and do little more than caress your hair. You must focus, though, on becoming one with the universe. Remove yourself from society and seek enlightenment.' All these things I heard were amazing and gave me cause for thought. I pondered them as I travelled further. I went an amazing distance, hearing fantastic proclamations from Zen masters and other incredible figures, and had travelled so far that I had returned to my point of departure. I stood there ruminating over what I had seen and heard when suddenly a darkness engulfed me and an entity swirling within an impenetrable cloud spoke in an ancient tone. 'I go by many names, all of which have been perverted. I am Prometheus, Amon, Beelzebub, Bile, Demogorgon, Haborym, Loki, Mictian, Moloch, Nergal, O-Yama, Pwcca, Rimmon, Samnu, Siva, T'an-mo, Tchort, Arawn, Baphomet, Lucifer, and so forth. You should believe me when I say that you should not listen to me at all. I am constantly searching, and I lie. I do not believe in truth.'

"So John, what do you think?"

John shakes his head with a disappointed air. "I don't think it was very well written...or researched for that matter."

"True, you are correct on that score but don't make the mistake of assuming that it does not have deep currents of thought or understanding. There are certain things in this world that people cannot conceive of or comprehend the relevance of until they have experienced the same lifestyle as the person relating any particular understanding. Geryon's parable will make more sense to you once you have reached that point of the path he treads now."

John feels a desire to berate the Shaman for demeaning his personal accumulation of experience and knowledge, but he is interrupted by Geryon's dance partner. She deftly slides into the booth next to him, smiles beguilingly, and tosses stray raven locks back from her face to expose fine ivory features. Her hand strays to his leg and strokes it lightly.

"Hello, Delilah," the Shaman hails her. "Leaving our boy so soon?"

She ignores his gibe, instead focusing her attention on John's eyes. Her hand slinks further up his leg, and as it moves closer to his groin he feels his cock grow to meet it halfway. His body seems trapped in time, unable to act in either a positive or negative way towards her sexual advances. Before he has time to respond, she unbuttons his pants and leans over to suck on his aroused member. John remains paralyzed in his seat. Oddly enough, he finds himself staring at the Shaman who simply raises his eyes in an exasperated manner and does nothing. John wants to say something to the Shaman, but the paralysis extends to his vocal chords. Ecstasy touches on every part of his body, building quickly and reducing his vision to nothing. His body transforms to an ethereal state, becoming nothing more than an intense sensation of pleasure without body or mind. Suddenly, whoosh, he cums into the girl's mouth with great force. He cannot help but think that her head should explode out the back from the velocity of it, but she simply pops back up into a sitting position and wipes her lips with the back of her hand. Her lipstick smears raggedly across her cheek, and somehow the effect created by that crimson splash works in contrast to her pale skin to give her an enticingly evil appearance. Against his own will, John feels the desire to bite her neck. She prevents this by standing up to leave. John's libido immediately deflates.

"So," the Shaman inquires again with a more direct tone. "What is happening between you and Geryon?"

Delilah throws her head back, nonchalantly, and laughs. "Oh, he is no more." And with that ominous pronouncement she jumps up and strides off toward the club's single exit. John and the Shaman glance at each other and then quickly rush to the back room, an alcove hidden from prying eyes by a high black curtain. The scene inside is gruesome. John halts in motion as he arrives, for there before him lies Geryon, sprawled shirtless on the floor amidst silk sheets and pillows. Geryon's oriental green dragon tattoo first grasps his attention as it stretches up his arm to end with its gaping mouth near his pectoral, but it is his blade that John notices next and cannot pry his eyes away from. Geryon's knife sticks surreally out from the nipple of the left breast in a portrait of the doomed melancholic from German literature, and the blood pouring from the wound appears to be a part of the tattoo, disgorged as fiery dragon's vomit across the visible ribs of Geryon's abdomen. John's mind refuses to believe Geryon has been murdered. He tells himself that people do not kill each other in this society, but then he remembers what he thought as he gazed down upon his grandfather's corpse. He had realized that he has difficulty believing in death in general. It is too terrible a concept for him. John's thoughts return to Delilah. He cannot accept the fact that he had just received oral sex from the woman who had taken Geryon's own blade and plunged it into his chest to the hilt. What would possess such a person to kill another, particularly when that one was a lover? John looks over at his companion. The Shaman does not seem surprised at the situation. He places his hand upon John's shoulder and says, "I knew this would happen. It is an inevitable occurrence along the path." Then he lets a somber silence invades again, but anger rises in John as hears those words.

"What do you mean it was inevitable? The fact that he should die is inevitable? I don't want to walk your path if it means I am going to die. Fuck you!"

The Shaman roughly grabs both of John's triceps and squeezes. "I can relate to your feelings, John, but there is something that I must tell you, something that I must ingrain in your head. Let us take our leave, and I will help you understand."

As the Shaman leads John towards the exit, the patrons of the bar watch their progress with thin slit eyes. John cannot help but sense some form of anger directed

Jean-Paul Corriveau

his way, as if he were the one to have embedded the knife in Geryon's chest. He does not understand it, and an indignant fury rises inside his brain. He wants to shove the Shaman away and scream like a banshee at the insensitive people around the room, but his sense of decorum stops him. The Shaman seems to pick up on his emotions and attempts to placate him with more talk.

"You must realize that the path to wisdom and understanding is filled with sorrow and pain. All who walk the path accept this fact. This pain is individual and cannot be projected upon or taken up by any other person. It would not be right. It would demean the person who treads the path because it would keep that person from truly experiencing the journey. The personal experience is the point of the endeavor. I understand your anger. Truly, I do. It is this desire to know why, which can never be satisfied, but in the meantime requires so much sacrifice. I also understand your need to rise above it. I wrote a journal entry once concerning this. Maybe it will help you grasp what I am saying."

'Right now I feel this heated anger, this protean dissonance, welling up deep in my soul. It expands and pushes and stretches my flesh to the tearing point, making me desire to run and traverse endless miles with blinding speed and pound upon everything before me until this fury subsides to lay a dormant weight nestled among my entrails. Yet I am restrained. This invisible hand holds me down and sustains my wrath between ethereal fingers. I claw and gouge and attempt to struggle loose but to no avail. I scream and bite, but it feels nothing. This force is as intangible as laughter, and still the pain grows inside.'

"You feel this hand upon you now, don't you, John?"

John nods slowly. His eyes star at the cold cement floor of the club.

"It is okay to feel that way, John. It is how we all feel. And believe me, the pressure does relax its grip from time to time. At present, though, you are too new to the experience of death. Your reactions are rather extreme. That is to be expected. You need to realize that death is an inevitable aspect of existence. It is a sad occurrence, and yet coincidently a happy one as well. Death provides life with meaning. Death renews the world. Death also releases a person from daily strife...plus, there are many kinds of death. You are only thinking in terms of the physical. There are psychological deaths as well. What you saw tonight is the latter. Geryon did not really die, John. What you saw with your eyes was a metaphor. We, who are Outsiders, do not always die in the conventional sense, but rather ascend to another state of being."

96

"This isn't going to make much sense to you now, but I will try to get it across as best as I can. You see, almost every person starts out their life dead, which is why we call them 'deadmen'. They do not realize that they exist in this state of death because they have been told the lie that they are alive. Now, this part will sound oxymoronic at first, but it is not. Just follow along and understand that the same word may be used to describe opposing ideas. In order to rise out of the state of death, an Outsider must die. This is what happened to Geryon. Dying destroys the elements that make people lifeless in their existence. Dying becomes the transition to a state of living death, and then from there to actual life. It is a process that has been incorrectly written about by deadmen in the various horror stories passed down over the last couple centuries. From their perspective, the process is frightening and unnatural. Frightening, yes, but unnatural, no. The problem being that they cannot understand why it must occur, and they write their tales to direct people away from a process they find horrifying and painful. In turn, the process becomes portrayed as inherently evil to justify their lack of understanding and fear. What we, Outsiders, have done is reclaim these stories in order to learn more about ourselves and our evolution. We can also use them to gain pride and guidance."

"Take werewolf stories for example. Those people who turn into animals when the moon is full represent an allegorical way to describe the party person who stays out all night drinking, doing drugs, having sex. Werewolves represent the first, most childlike stage along the path. This is the state that Geryon is currently leaving and that you are about to enter. It is a state of heightened sensuality and submission to carnal desires. It is a lust for life, a drive to experience one's physical and mental potential. In the stories, the person is still considered by deadmen as a living being, though we Outsiders would still say dead being because no death will have occurred to the person until the end of this stage. The werewolf himself though wants to believe that he is further along the path than he really is. He is in a state of denial and wants to believe he is in the third stage. Therefore, he assumes a name that will fool the deadmen but not other Outsiders. That is why David assumed the name Geryon. He wanted to think his reckless freedom made him more than he was. He wanted to feel powerful and wild. Because of this, most werewolves are also killers. Their youth and inexperience causes them to run out of control, an action which unfortunately instills more fears in the deadmen, and the werewolf will revert to animal drives with no thought whatsoever. That is why they must die. They must die to arrest their uncontrolled carnal tendencies, as well as appease the deadmen's need for justice."

"The second stage, then, is the first time that Outsiders rise from the grave. Vampire tales have typically described this stage. Stories about night stalkers that

Jean-Paul Corriveau

suck the blood of the 'living' actually depict the initial turning of the Outsider from the illusions of the deadmen. The vampire feeds off of the cultural twists and turns of the dead world while simultaneously turning away from society and the false light of day. Vampires strive to create a new lifestyle. They seek an existence of beauty and truth and power and passion…as well as terror. From here, the Outsider may or may not die again to reach stage three because their actions are actually more refined and obscure than in the previous stage, though that may be difficult to tell as their sexuality is also rather strong."

"Stage three resides in tales told about the devil, the fall of the brightest angel. The devil was thrown out of Heaven because he cried, 'non serviam', or I will not serve, to God. God, of course, represents the dictates of society. The brightest angel, in turn, represents the most fearless, creative, and intelligent individuals in a society. Devils, therefore, are those innovators that society seeks to repress to maintain docility in its other subjects. Devils, themselves, serve no society, religion, or government, and they seek only to find understanding based on true living. They seek to know who they are by being everything under the sun."

"Now one might think that the stage of devil would be the final stage, but that is not the case. From here, devils may evolve to stage four, Deadmen would classify this stage as godhood (or in some circles, magician ship) if they were willing to accept it. And only a few Outsiders manage to understand the difference between this stage and the previous, though the ones that accept it as godhood do so with certain restrictions. This stage is very similar to the concept of the Buddha in Tantric religion. A god's purpose is to attempt to help others in the world evolve and reach a state of Nirvana. As I am currently in this stage, I am a little hesitant to discuss it more with you. Suffice to say, that it is a state of being that is non-being at the same time. Do not ask me to explain it further."

The Shaman throws open the exit door at that moment, and a brilliant shaft of light bursts into the outer hall of the club. John holds his hand up to shield his eyes, but at the prompting of the Shaman steps out into the morning. The club stands on the desolate western outskirts of town. A sign above the door states that it is called the Worm Hole. To the west, John can barely see the mountains across the yellowish-brown plains. They are covered in a haze, and only the shadowed outlines of the peaks poke forth, otherworldly and mysterious. The Shaman pulls at John's sleeve and leads him down the road away from the club and the town.

"You see, John," he starts again. "Death is nothing to be afraid of. Death promotes change and helps our world and those in it to grow and evolve. But you must beware. There are dark warriors along the path as well as spiritual warriors. Dark warriors are Outsiders who have become caught up in the traps I mentioned earlier. Dark warriors have become mired in their progress along the path and no longer continued to evolve…and that makes them very vicious. These are dangerous creatures, John. These beings are beyond the zombies of the world. They are the ghouls and liches of the undead mythology, and you should beware them at all costs. They will drag you down with them."

The Shaman pauses for a second and stares off into space. Then he resumes with a flip of his hand. "But enough of this metaphysical babbling. Your head must be spinning from it all. I have just one more thing to say."

John's head is indeed spinning rapidly despite his having sobered most of the way up in the past couple hours. It helps him to look off into the distance instead of directly down at his moving feet. The field stretches out to the mountains with numerous bumps and hills rising skyward to stimulate the mind, and squat leafless bushes and prairie grass grow in pattern less patches across the landscape. A profusion of holes dots the area where a score of prairie dogs stand on their hind legs. Each of the little rodents remains perfectly still and stares into the sky with a glazed expression. Each manages to appear both cute and pathetic, simultaneously, and each also looks as lifeless as stone.

"Consider those prairie dogs to be your average person," the Shaman commands. "They stare blindly into nothing, dead to their environment except for the approach of predators. They are the sentinels to oblivion. They are weak and paranoid, and they tear up their habitat for that is what they have been trained to do. Destruction is sometimes fine in the human growing process, but when you take destruction out of life, out of its grounded state, and place it within a system, be it political, religious, or otherwise, than problems arise. Systems are concepts, not living beings, and as such they cannot truly learn and mature. Thus, their entanglement with destruction becomes the mundane perpetuated. Nothing short of the obliteration of the world will stop a system's tendency towards destruction. In that lies the evil of capitalism and other American systems, as well as those across the globe."

The Shaman's good hand grabs John's elbow to punctuate his next words.

Jean-Paul Corriveau

"So you see, to return to my allegory, those prairie dogs will continue to tunnel across the plains until they consume it completely. Their actions are no different than when capitalists continue to mine, spill oil, chop down forests, and deplete the ozone until this world is a ball of dust. There is no limit to the destruction caused by a system's existence. They are befuddled. You need to ask yourself what force it is that pushes you and others toward systemization. What force is it that took the hippies of the 60's and mutated them? What force is it that perverts the turnings of the sacred hoop? Consider your job. Why does corporate work place a box around your mind to prevent you from thinking and seeing? Why is it that you cannot let your mind wander or rise beyond mundane thought without striking one of the walls of this box? Why?"

John's head has begun to feel like it is striking against some invisible barrier in front of him. He has taken in too much information in the past few hours. His legs go wobbly, and he leans against the Shaman who has undergone a mystical metamorphosis into an elderly man in a long flowing robe with a lantern. He has transformed into some ancient, mountainous hermit. The Hermit takes a clear plastic bag containing a sheet of white paper with perforated squares and a black metal hunting knife and shoves them into John's pocket. John barely notices this action and does nothing to resist. The Hermit then draws John's attention along the stretch towards the mountains. The white horse from the previous night gallops toward the pair of them from some unknown location and despite its speed John senses that it will not attempt to hurt them. The flames in its eyes blaze less dangerously.

"Time to fire walk," the Hermit whispers, enigmatically, and he helps the non-resistant John onto the horse's back. John stares down at the Hermit who smiles in return. After a moment, he begins to slowly fade away. The outer edges of his body become wavy like water flowing across glass, and the colors of his clothes and skin lighten and pale until his translucence reveals the shapes of grass and ground behind him. At this point, the Hermit addresses John one last time.

He states, "tonight will seem like a dream to you in the future. But over time the memories of what you have learned will seep back into your consciousness. Do not deny them!"

And then he disappears completely from sight.

The horse uses that moment to streak off across the plains. The air created by its speed whips into John's face, exhilarating him. It turns his thoughts away from the

100

Hermit and Geryon and everything else, except the sensation that he feels at this very moment. John notices his body energizing due to the movement of the horse. He feels its shift into life. It is a tremendous experience. John becomes so wrapped up in the feeling that he stays unconcerned about the horse's helter skelter movement. The two of them race to the state border crossing back into Colorado, back past his point of departure. Things will be different this time. The revelation is invigorating.

John understands that he is evolving. And what is more…he accepts it.

Into the Night

Part I: On the Prowl

I know you are out there. I can smell you. The scent of nervousness, fear, and excitement carries across these rolling hills like a tepid evening breeze. It awakens the beast within me. I know I will find you. I can hear the clamoring of your voices as you hide deep in the recesses of your pitiful shelters. Your cries vie for attention, and I will home in upon any random one, woe unto you, with darkness covering my approach and slaver dripping from my curled lips. You are all sheep, I say, a pathetic group of animals whose lives mean little across the endless span of time. Just stand there, helpless, in your meaty frames and shake for I am the creature designed to feed off of your weaknesses. Huddling together in herds does nothing to protect you from my attack.

The drive always seems so blasted eternal. I should just up and move to Boulder instead of making the fifteen or twenty-minute trek every Friday. I am sick of dealing with the fucking traffic, and the cops, and having to locate a place to park my car for the night. What a pain! At least the scenery is not too bad. One minute there is urban sprawl, with the bright lights of strip malls, the colossal twenty-four screen movie theaters, and the gaily-colored banners of the Butterfly Pavilion, and the next there is western landscape streaking out into the airy spaciousness of the foothills that lead to the vale that is Boulder. I must say that I dig gazing at the setting sun as it descends behind the three jutting points that are collectively known as the Flatirons. The sight does something inside of me, though if you want to know what exactly I doubt I would be able to explain it to you.

Yet, I can say why I am departing from Denver every weekend. It is a matter of going somewhere earthy. I need to get away from city and plain and smog and let my legs run free among the hedonism surrounding the University of Colorado. I need to be able to let my hair down and go wild in one of the last bastions of nationally supported illegality.

You can understand that, right?

I mean we all have these urges welling up inside of us. They come on like hunger pangs, except that they do not stay knotted up in the center of one's abdomen. Rather, they spread out in little tendrils of electricity and build and build until the entire body feels wracked with this sort of nervous energy. It takes only a couple of hours, in my case, before these urges consume me. Then, the tugging begins, and I feel as if someone has attached a thin rope to my stomach and pulls on it from some distant location. I feel compelled to travel to whatever place has summoned me so that I can alleviate these uncomfortable sensations.

Lately, the rope always seems to end in Boulder.

I look to my left and grimace. The Native American has been staring at me again. I hate that. He simply sits there in my passenger seat with his head tilted slightly and looks at me with those shiny bulbous eyes. He acts like he knows everything about me. Yet, I know practically nothing about him; I do not even know what freaking tribe he is. Maybe it is Ute or Arapahoe, but I cannot be sure. His look is pretty typical. A white eagle feather has been tied to a strand of his thick black hair, and the hair hangs down to his shoulders and covers the top of his tanned hide jerkin. He wears a pair of hide pants to match the top. His feet never show. I do not know if he even has feet, as he has only appeared to me in the car after dusk.

"Stop that," I yell. "Quit freaking staring at me!"

Of course, this exclamation proves ineffectual.

I consider striking him with the back of my fist, but I know from prior experience that this action will not provide me with a positive result either. My hand will pass right through his body and will strike the semi-soft cushion of the passenger seat headrest without hindrance. I have given up attempting to determine whether this annoying apparition is actually a ghost from a past life, a guardian spirit or Manito, or some sort of conjuration from my subconscious brought on by stress or drugs or whatnot.

"You should not be so angry, grandson. You are throwing yourself out of balance."

I glance over at him and laugh. "I am a force of nature, grandfather. I cannot be out of balance."

The Native American shakes his head and raises a finger in exclamation. "Yes, this is true. Nature itself cannot be out of balance...but you are not Nature in its entirety." With this, he pokes me in the arm with his finger. "You are only a part of Nature, and as such you can be moved away from the center. Right now, you have a demon inside of you, and that you need to overcome."

I do not stop to analyze why he is solid when he touches me but incorporeal when I try to touch him. Instead, I seek to upset him. "Yeah, well, that is what I am going to do right now. I am going to take a lot of drugs and get a little crazy, and I am going to force the demon, back down into his pit. What do you fucking think of that?"

"I believe your use of the sacred plants lacks in ritual."

"Oh do you know? What a shame. I guess I'm going to have to settle for the simple fun that the hallucinogenic effects give me. Just take a little ride, you know?"

The Native American shakes his head again, appearing rather distressed. The hairs bristle up on the back of my neck, and I realize that I am sick of him patronizing me like this. Before I can stop myself, I throw a hard punch toward his jaw. My hand, of course, passes directly through his head and connects with the plastic segment between the front and back doors on his side. His head continues shaking around my outstretched arm.

I pull my hand back and return it to the steering wheel. As I do, my sixth sense goes off, and I turn to notice a car passing me on the left. In it, an elderly husband and wife gawk at me with horrified expressions. They seem so nice and domestic. I snarl at them, flick my tongue in and out, and make intimidating gestures with my hands. This causes the woman to shriek. The look on her face makes me laugh, and the man reacts by stepping on the gas. I turn to say something snotty to the Native American about the incident, but I find that he has disappeared. Oh well. At least I won't have to put up with him for the rest of the trip.

The final descent into Boulder is vastly impressive. Highway 36 drops down what is probably a three percent grade into a lower vale at the foot of the mountains where it shoots straight north through town as 28th street. The first things that one notices are the university dormitories. The two yellow buildings stand about fifteen stories high just to the right of Highway 36 on the south side of town and are easily the tallest in the county. Various colors shine from the windows, most prominent being the eerie purplish haze of a black light, and many of the windows bear banners and flyers proclaiming all important teenage messages such as "Coors Beer", "The Dead Rule", and "Party Animal". The rest of the town consists of mostly two-story homes and apartments, except for the various malls located here and there, the university, and the Hill. It is the cluster of lights from these buildings that manages to create a faery like effect as one descends into the vale.

The Hill is my immediate destination tonight. This commercial zone covers about a two-block area on 13th Street just west of the university and south a jog from the big outdoor mall on Pearl Street. I really groove on the Hill, despite the fact that there are those who consider it pretentious. Three decent record stores can be found on the Hill, as well as a number of basic food establishments, shops, and entertainment facilities. It is the type of place that one can find near any institution for higher education. It is where the college students typically frequent to obtain their essentials. The big difference, here, being that the Hill is also a hangout for hippy wannabes who believe in the Boulder hype, and on most nights of the week one can find between twenty to thirty homeless looking youths hanging out on the corners and benches. As much as I find their posturing ludicrous in many cases, I love to walk down the sidewalk and study the crazy fashions and hairstyles of the kids who have tried to adopt the sixties ideal as they believe it to have been lived.

First, I turn off on Baseline Road and cruise up towards the Flatirons before taking a right onto 14th Street. From there, it does not take me long to arrive at the pay parking lot that is free after six at night. I pull into an empty spot near the alley

Jean-Paul Corriveau

beside the pizza joint and sit there a moment listening to the end of "Cosmik Debris" which is the current song playing on the mixed tape I chose for this evening. Beautiful! Zappa has style, despite the message he propounds.

I am much calmer now that I have arrived. Driving around Colorado always makes me uptight for some reason, and the Native American does not seem to realize how stressful traveling the highways can be. Maybe next time I will try to explain it to him. He always wants to pin my mood off on generalized distress.

Anyway, I head down the alley and turn onto the bottom part of the L shaped avenues that form the Hill. The smell of pizza wafts out from the open door to the pizza joint, and the odor is so tantalizing that I cannot resist. I step in for a moment to buy a slice of cheese and wolf it down before walking to the street corner and turning to the right.

The air is balmy tonight, and the hippy hopefuls are out in droves. A group of four obvious high school kids stand near the gutter talking lethargically. They wear dingy, oversized jeans, hooded hemp pullovers, and big brown boots with strategically placed holes in the fabric. Their hair has been fashioned into clumpy dreadlocks. If it were not for the difference in their hair color, one would think that they were clones. I stride past them and immediately stumble across some veteran wannabes, two males and a female with a black Labrador retriever. They expertly lounge against the front façade of the video arcade, having stuck their greasy, panted legs out into the walkway, and they stare up at the evening sky with wondrous expressions. The relaxation they evince does not erase the lines of exhaustion that crease their faces. Even the dog raises a weary eye at me as I pass by, the red bandana tied around his neck doing nothing to make him look more cute or playful. Both guys manage to accomplish fading into the surrounding with great skill, but the girl has trouble sitting still. She hauls herself up off the ground and fidgets around, shaking her legs and wiping her hands upon the back of her jeans. I laugh inwardly. There must have been too much strychnine in the doses that I am guessing she bought off the street. She looks dirty and worn, yet I notice some of the youthful beauty working its way past the stench and filth of her current incarnation. Perhaps, it has to do with the white cotton tank top she wears sans bra. Her nipples poke through the thin material of the shirt and that erotic sight, combined with her tanned, bare arms and shoulders, evokes an image of fresh flowers and spice.

I decide not to dwell on her too long. She is not the one I am looking for, and I have somewhere I want to be.

I stroll another half block northward to my destination and turn left into the Fox Theater. Hunter S Thompson has agreed to make a special appearance in town tonight. I am not sure why, perhaps he is promoting his new book, or bored, or something, but I am not going to argue against his decision. I have wanted to meet the man since reading <u>Fear and Loathing in Las Vegas</u>, which is a book that makes me laugh louder than any other thing I've ever read or viewed. It is a totally killer piece of work, and I have hoped to have the chance to delve into the psyche of the man behind the piece for quite some time.

The Fox Theater is a two-room building for patrons: the entranceway includes a pizza order counter, two bathrooms, and a half-hexagonal bar against the far wall; the back room contains a stage where the performances take place and a second bar. The back room is arranged as a multiple level affair. The highest level is located by the two openings from the entranceway and circles around the room in the shape of the letter U. It gives the patrons the option of sitting on benches high against the sides of the walls or at tables separated from the lower levels by a black metal railing. Because of the soundboard situated at the base of the U in an enclosed box, there is only a limited amount of standing space on this level. Plus, short steps lead down on either side of the soundboard to the lower levels and require a certain amount of area be left open for traffic. The lower levels, on the other hand, are completely open spaces that sit directly in front of the stage—one behind and above the other so that the people standing in the front do not block the view of those further away.

A small crowd has gathered tonight to see Hunter. Approximately, thirty people mill about in the lower levels near the stage, and a few more than that have occupied the tables on either side of the room. The group is not what I expected, the majority of them appearing to be under twenty-five years in age. Freaking kids, I curse to myself. What is even worse is that most are dressed in khaki shorts, t-shirts promoting some spring break hotspot, and baseball caps worn bill forward. I feel as if I have walked into a chapter meeting for the collegiate republicans. The sight makes me ill. What do these shits think they are doing? Are these the "cool" yuppie kids out having an evening of debauchery with the nearest thing to the anti-Christ that they are willing to espouse? I can see it now. Come Monday morning they are going to walk into their business ethics class, and they are going to brag about meeting the big, bad Hunter S Thompson face to face. They are going to sit there and regale their not so cool yuppie friends, who spent Friday night playing trivial pursuit and listening to No Doubt, about how they partied hard with the master of craziness.

"Oh, you should have been there. I must have drunk like sixteen huge microbrews. I was so plastered. I got up on the stage and jumped onto Hunter's back, and he spun me around while we screamed at the top of our lungs. Wooohooo! It was really awesome. Too bad you were home, Friday, and not with us. You really missed out."

For a moment, I debate leaving and heading over to my friend's party early, but I stop myself. I came here hoping to obtain the psychological profile of one of the more influential writers of our time. I can still do that, I tell myself, and perhaps also add a bit to the profile I have worked up on the conservative, mundane types I generally avoid.

I resolve to stay and position myself behind the soundboard where the shadows cover my presence from the rest of the people in the room.

The herd is large, but I can smell the blood of the one I desire. I sense its heat out near the edge of the group. Enticing me. Summoning me. Crying to be released from all of life's misery and boredom. Slowly, I stalk forward allowing the gleam of my fangs to precede my body in the darkness. Fear coupled with stifled passion will help the little lamb to give into the warmth of my embrace.

I sense her loitering nearby before I actually know she is there. One moment I am watching the not-so-amusing antics of the people in the crowd who are waiting for Hunter to arrive (he is almost an hour late, go figure), and the next I spin my head to the right to find a dark-haired, Elvin girl hiding in the darkness behind the soundboard with me. My initial reaction is to consider her to be too mouse-like for consideration, like the stereotypical librarian, but that quickly proves itself a mischaracterization on my part. No, she is definitely a hybrid of some sort, and it is with a minor shock that I realize she is the one for tonight. She glances over at me through the edge of her thin-rimmed metal glasses, betraying the gypsy within her. Fine features, olive skin, mysterious eyes. She holds contact for a fraction of a second and then pretends to return her attention to the spotlighted stage. The pursing of her lips gives her thoughts away, though. I continue to observe her and see that she has pulled her hair back into the professional style of the career girl and wears the double-breasted suit of a man. Had she put her hair in a ponytail or not had fine facial features or slight curves on her chest, I might have mistaken her for a feminine male. But I can see that she is a woman, and I find her gender crossing tendencies intriguing. I smile devilishly and make it obvious that I continue to watch her.

Hunter decides to amble on stage at that moment, amidst the cheers of his youthful admirers. He plops himself down on a metal folding chair in the center of the stage and begins fumbling with the microphone and the complimentary jar and glass of water on a little wooden table to his left. He appears to be completely intoxicated. After a few moments, he mumbles something incoherent into the microphone. The crowd glances around at each other confused. They had expected some paragon of inebriation, not some actual drunkard. After about ten minutes of nonsensical speech spewing from Hunter's mouth, one brave youth near the stage decides to attract Hunter's attention. He spends a few minutes frantically waving his arms and yelling, and eventually Hunter quiets down and swings his heavy gaze around to stare at the boy. The youth wastes no time asking the question that he probably spent all day contemplating how to word.

"Hunter, do you believe that the values promoted by our society have put us in decline? Are we heading to destruction, or do you see some other possibility in store for us? And do you have a solution in mind?"

"Well…" Hunter breathes and then pauses to collect his thoughts. The youth does not give Hunter the chance to continue, as the boy suddenly remembers that he has another part of his question that he needs to ask.

"And do you think that they should allow eighteen year olds to legally drink?"

A cheer rises up from the crowd, and Hunter's body jolts backward. He steadies himself awkwardly before gazing angrily out at the crowd. He seems to realize that his fans here are nothing but imbeciles looking for the ultimate party, and one can see from his expression that he has determined he should give them what they want. Hunter immediately kicks over the microphone, which gives a sharp bang as it hits the floor, and then he falls off of his chair. While attempting to right himself, he grabs hold of a plastic fan behind him, for support, and starts to slam it around on the stage and kick it until little pieces of plastic go flying in random directions. The crowd continues to cheer for their party god.

"This is pathetic," I growl.

The dark haired, Elvin girl's mouth breaks into a smirk, but she keeps her focus on the stage.

Hunter's drunken sideshow continues for about a half an hour before the club owner walks out on stage and assists him back into his seat. With the owner's aid, more questions are fielded by Hunter, who replies with his characteristic mumble, telling uninspiring tales about his drunken exploits in Aspen, until one young man's question finally jolts him into meaningfulness.

"Considering the recent death of Allen Ginsberg, what do you think about the fact that all our icons are disappearing? Do you have any comment about that?"

Hunter stares directly at the young man in the tan, tweed jacket, and a fire blazes suddenly behind his eyes. His jaw trembles slightly, and it is with a burst of disgust that he volleys forth the following reply.

"Why don't you get your own damn icons to worship? Quit looking to the past!"

For me, that one statement redeems what I had up until then considered to be the apparent ruin of a man. It proves that a sliver of the strength and drive which had once energized Hunter still exists in that crumbling body today, and it shows that the movement his concepts spawned has not been a transient endeavor. To my surprise, I feel like applauding.

The dark haired, Elvin girl speaks to me abruptly and says, "This has got to be pretty much over. What say we retire to the front bar and have a drink?"

"That sounds like an excellent idea," I agree and flash another toothy grin at her. She smiles back with a slight quiver of apprehension that stokes the fires within me. Is she nervous from having made the first move and appeared too forward, or is her timid nature affected by my bravado? I gaze into her eyes, and the brightness I see there, along with the way her pupils widen, tells me that I have nothing to worry about. I have already succeeded in charming her. Her nervousness is part of the spell I have cast, and from here on I simply need to let things evolve naturally to complete the seduction.

"What do you think of Hunter?" I ask as we take our first sips off of a couple of Flat Tires.

"He's a buffoon," she replies readily. "He seems to be nothing but a washed up drunk with nothing important to say."

"Oh, I don't know. I think that comment about finding our own icons was rather well put. Could it be that your opinion has been affected by the type of crowd he drew?"

"Perhaps," she acquiesces, "I think there are too many idiots in our genera-tion...too many people who buy into what they are told is cool."

"Yeah, people need to move forward and create their own styles and beliefs, not try to live something that they weren't a part of in the first place."

The beer slides easily down my throat; I have emptied the glass without re-membering having imbibed most of it. Before I can set down my empty mug, a tall blonde bartendress in a tight white t-shirt and jeans places a new one in front of me and grabs the old one. She winks knowingly, then walks away, performing a cute little spin on the ball of her foot as she does so.

My drinking companion pretends to be thinking intently. She stares at the wall for a few moments, and then she re-initiates the conversation.

"So...are you familiar with psychological theory?"

I nod in way of reply and struggle to maintain a casual expression. Every part of my body has become alert and observant. She has moved the discussion to the second level. On the surface her question may seem simple and harmless, but really she has mouthed a segue way that can lead to a line of questioning which, if handled improperly on my end, could spell disaster. I quickly decide to take control of the topic and move it into a more favorable direction.

"I've read a lot of Freud," I say. "I believe he was a brilliant man, but he got too caught up trying to push certain concepts. If something is untenable don't stick with it just because it conforms to your ideology."

I pause and mentally pat myself on the back. The statement is wonderfully vague and non-confrontational. I can argue on Freud's behalf or against it. Now, the pressure lies on my companion, who must contrive some equally vague analysis or actually speak her convictions. Fortunately for me, she chooses the latter.

"Yes, that whole idea about penis envy is so chauvinistic."

"The Oedipus and Electra complexes," I mumble and take another swig. I relax and let myself fall passively in line with her personal judgements.

"Freud was a fool for basing his concepts of women off of men. As if women are simply the antithesis of men. As if men are the rule, are the norm, to which everything in the universe must be compared!"

A budding feminist, I decide. Some insecurity is making her speak so angrily, and that makes her easy prey.

My companion carries the conversation for the next half hour. I break in occasionally with some poignant comment that allows her to proselytize on various subjects, and she feels quite pleased that someone acknowledges her personal beliefs. It pleases me as well that what she has to say is interesting and deftly rationalized. Her intelligence further arouses my lust.

I begin to slide Aleister Crowley into the discussion when I notice that the bartendress has been standing nearby listening. She makes it obvious that she wants to speak.

"Ya know, you two are one of the coolest couples I've seen in here in awhile."

"Oh, we are not a couple," I reply. I make sure that my voice carries the proper amount of embarrassment.

The blonde does little to conceal her pleasure at that announcement. Glancing back at my companion, I have a difficult time determining how she feels about this new development. Her face has turned rigid as stone.

"Well, you two sure look like you should be together. And the way you were talking. Gawd, you're both so smart."

The softness returns to my companion's face. She thanks the blonde for her compliment.

"I'm Janie," the blonde states with a strange flourish of her arms.

"Violet," my companion returns graciously.

I give my name in turn, and the two girls begin making small talk about where they live and how they go to school at the university and what they study. I zone out at this point and pretend to direct my attention to the crowd. I am amazingly unsure of myself now. Could the bartendress be a lesbian? I had not gotten that impression from watching her behind the bar, but then that is not exactly the ideal location for examining someone. I get somewhat miffed at this point. This is not what I wanted. Violet is the girl for tonight. I am sure about this. No interference should be occurring. Rapidly, I begin to conceive of a plan for regaining control of the situation, but suddenly both girls rest their hands on my right forearm. Their touch catches me by surprise.

"We've decided to go back to Violet's place to smoke a little doobie," the blonde informs me.

"That's great," I smile and adopt my friend to the world attitude.

The blonde has apparently reached the end of her shift, and she crawls out from behind the bar to entwine her arms in both of ours and lead us out of the Fox towards Violet's Buick. A short ride and five blocks later we arrive at the worn down, brown, one floor house that Violet rents with a fellow university student. She fumbles for the key and utters a hasty, "the place is a mess," before ushering us inside. I notice that her body quivers with excitement and nervousness.

The living room attached to the outer door manages to impress me. Only two couches line either side of the room, but paintings and prints with a striking appearance adorn most of the space on three of the walls. Violet's roommate has a rather interesting style, I think, assuming that Violet herself did not do these, though she made no mention of this talent. Each painting differs greatly from the others in terms of color scheme and visual theme, but they all utilize a surreal look patterned after Salvador Dali. They are what Hallucinogenic Toreador would be if it were a multilayered collage. I plop down on the left couch in order to relax and scrutinize them better.

After a few moments, the girls return from a room located behind a door on the far wall and settle onto the opposite couch. They have brought a tin of marijuana, a lighter, and some rolling papers with them. Janie announces that she is rather skilled at rolling joints, so she proceeds to pull out a quarter bag from the tin and prepare the fun. I mention that I would prefer to use my bat, and I pull out my stealth hitter from my back pocket. Violet nods her head understandingly and tosses a different quarter bag to me so that I can immediately light up with my black metal piece. I happily do so.

Violet seems overjoyed at the way her little party is turning out. She gleefully explains how she obtained the sensemila from a good friend of hers who travels to Mexico regularly and how it is the purest breed. I have to admit that it has a nice taste and packs quite a punch. Janie vocalizes the same thing as she takes a number of drags off of one of the joints she has rolled. I watch as the two of them suck down five joints in quick succession. They seem to have an insatiable hunger for the weed, a fact that gears up my libido again, but aside from that I cannot say that they have anything in common.

You see, my stoned mind recognizes the delicious dichotomy right away.

On the one hand, there is Janie, the husky, blonde from New York City. She has little formal education, and probably thinks that Freud is the name of some artsy band, but her street knowledge and social skills are extremely honed. She loves to communicate and interact. Also, her body has more curves on it than a winding mountain trail.

On the other hand, there is Violet, a black-haired waif born and bred in Boulder. Her strong intelligence is inarguable, but it is placed within a body that is lithe and youthful, almost genderless. These two factors have apparently created a discomfort in here concerning strangers. She desires friendship, but her mind tells her that she is different from others and easily misunderstood. This makes her hesitant, socially, but she blames her awkwardness on her looks and intelligence alone. It is sad, but also rather endearing.

Looking at these two and their complementary traits, I realize that I could not have asked for a more perfect match.

Janie, in the meantime, has become rather sensual with Violet now that the pot has fully affected her. She strokes Violet's bare arm and slowly kisses her neck.

I had been expecting this.

Suddenly, the Native American appears beside me and places a desperate hand upon my arm, and I realize that it is the first time he has appeared to me outside of the car. What does it mean? Why is he here? A twinge across my body makes me realize that I do not really care why. I feel my blood boil and sneer up at him, but he simply gazes at me with those sad, bulbous eyes before fading away as quickly as he came. I immediately forget about him. My dick has started pressing against the inside of my jeans.

With flames licking my entire body, I stand up and cross over to the other couch.

The sensation is beyond compare—to feel the liquid running over my chin and down my throat. I can do nothing but howl at the silver and black sky. The moon hangs brightly above me like a spotlight on a stage, and it illuminates my victory for the heavens. I am dead center. Arrooooo!

Janie throws her arms around me and gives me an enthusiastic hug. I plant my lips firmly against hers, marveling at the fact that though we both performed cunnilingus on Violet at the same time I can better taste her cum upon Janie's mouth. Janie separates and gives me one final wave before running towards her apartment. She yells out that I should get her phone number from Violet, so that I can call her. I feel relieved that she has been considerate enough to provide me with a reasonable excuse for not getting in touch with her again. As much as I liked her and enjoyed the sex, this had been a one-time deal. It is better for both of our lifestyles.

I think about Violet left asleep on the couch. What would she think about this tomorrow? Would she even remember it? I let the thought slip out of my mind. It is time to be heading to my friend's party.

Jean-Paul Corriveau

Rod shares a house on 41st Street with seven other, established hippies. Once every month or two, usually during a full moon or Solstice, they decide to host a party for all their tribe. It is a gala affair with tons of music and drugs and vegan dishes. No pleasure gets forgotten at this event.

I parallel park in front of a house that sits two down from my friend's abode. It amazes me how dark and quiet the outside of his place looks as I walk up to it. One would never guess that a full-blown party was happening inside. The front doorway to the house is located at the head of the drive behind the Gremlin that never seems to move and a stationary camper. As I open the door, light floods out onto the first, immobile vehicle betraying a faded green paint job and spreading rust.

Hot, humid air blasts across my body. It feels like a modern day sweat lodge, and I look inside to see a variety of unfamiliar people conversing and eating while standing or sitting around the two couches that are situated to form a ninety de-gree angle with each other down the middle of the room. Most of the illumination comes from the five humungous fish tanks that have been scattered about between a veritable jungle of plants and indoor trees. The phosphorescent glow emanating from the tanks throws bizarre shadows across the walls and gives each person present an otherworldly appearance. I smile gleefully. This is exactly how I like my evenings to start out—with a mystical shift out of the mundane into a universe…somewhere else.

Rod does not seem to be hanging out in the front room, so I glance quickly down the hallway on my left. No lights are on in the bedrooms down the hall, and the doors are shut. I decide that he is most likely not in that direction and walk along the hook to the right and head for the basement stairs via the kitchen. As I pass through the open space connecting the front room and the kitchen, an area that is technically meant to be a dining room, I have to maneuver around a colorful hippy garbed gypsy style, replete with bandana and black velvet vest. He sits cross-legged on the floor and performs an I Ching reading for two young wannabe girls who have dressed themselves in torn jeans, the ubiquitous hemp shirts, and Birkenstock sandals and who look a little too clean compared to the rest of the crowd here tonight. The gypsy appears comfortable playing the role of an eastern European nomad while tell-ing fortunes with a device that gained ascendance in a place thousands of miles away on the globe. I snort and think about how postmodernism takes on rather strange forms in the nineties.

The imitation gypsy throws two gold coins onto a mat. The coins are etched in great detail with a star on one side representing heads and a box on the other rep-resenting tails. The mat has the semi-ornate new-age decorations of something that came from a store bought kit. I find the capitalistic aspect of this occult exhibition rather disturbing. First, in the fact that the gypsy does not use the ancient method of the yarrow sticks for determining the hexagrams, and second, for the fact that these

114

girls will be so impressed with his "occult" knowledge and the (I sense it will come soon) fashionable exposition on the yin-yang that he has pieced together from different, drug-addled conversations he has held at various parties, thereby continuing the spread of misinformation to other ignorant rebel children. The outcome of this particular interaction will yet again prove to be a continuation of the sad, direction lacking repetition of half knowledge that most mundanes perpetuate, even the supposedly open minded ones. Hunter's words reverberate through my head, once more, about finding our own idols, and I look down at the trio with a mixture of pity and anger.

Fortunately, my disgust turns to delight as I round the corner and find every inch of the kitchen covered in blue and red clay bowls and dishes. Each bowl is filled to the rim with vegan delights, and I immediately notice the lovely odor of a spicy curry rising from one. All manner of beans, including lentils, form a multicolored batch in another. A plate of apple bread sits half eaten in the middle of the banquet as well. I grab a thin slice of pita, dunk it into a smooth olive colored dip that has attracted my notice, and wolf it down. The munchies brought about by my earlier sexual encounter and cannabis smoking have decided to wrack my body in full force after tasting the flavorful dip, which turns out to be avocado, so I forego all etiquette and shovel handfuls of the various vegan dishes into my mouth without hesitation. I forget to even savor the taste. It does not take long for me to realize how much of a pig I am being. I decide to finish quickly, and after glancing over all the bowls, I choose a plump mushroom marinated in a homemade blend to be the coup de grace for my feast.

"Hey, man," Rod calls out suddenly from my right. "You made it!"

I swallow the mushroom and throw my arms around my friend. He has on his torn jeans and favorite ice blue tie-dye shirt with the swimming dolphins and crystals. His beard and hair are growing out again, and they surround his face in a tangled mess of brown.

"Of course, dude," I happily reply, "would I boge on your trip?"

"Nah, I know you wouldn't. Man, you're just in time. The band is setting up to play, and we have the chance to get relaxed before they do."

Rod heads off down the staircase to the basement, not waiting to see if I will follow. I do, of course, and as I descend into the murky darkness I become temporarily overwhelmed by the odor of unshaven and unwashed bodies. This happens to be one of the few things that detract from these events as far as I am concerned. The rancorous smell of moist armpit is not one of the most pleasant experiences, but at least, one adjusts to it rather quickly. By the time I reach the bottom of the staircase, I no longer notice the smell. We walk through the small antechamber that is the first room of the basement and has the bathroom located under the stairs and pass into the adjacent hall that has Rod's room directly off of it to the right. Down to the left, the band has started tuning their acoustic guitars under the one sun lamp illuminating the area. That room forms most of the basement and is where I will spend most of my time this evening.

From the sounds of the tuning, it appears that Rod and I have at least ten minutes to hang loose before the duo will start to play.

Rod plops down on a mattress that he has shoved in the corner as a makeshift bed and grabs a bong, while I situate myself on the floor nearby with my back supported by the wall. He fills the bowl with some of his choice stash before passing the bong over to me in typical hippy host fashion. I wait a few minutes as he searches for a lighter, but once he locates one I light right up. I take a nice long drag off the tube and blissfully realize that the effects hit me immediately, probably because of my heavy usage earlier. Rod takes his turn, giving me the chance to gaze at the room's decorations. He has assembled a motley assortment of tie-dyed sheets, Jimi Hendrix posters, pictures of not-so-esoteric symbols (at least nowadays) for use with a black light, and photographs of random idyllic nature sites. I particularly take in a painting of blue-skinned Vishnu holding a lotus flower in his upper left hand.

"I can understand Shiva having multiple arms, but why give them to the other gods?" I wonder. Then I feel like slapping myself for asking such a stupid question.

Outside the door, the broken melodies of the band doing final testing on their instruments float down the hall. It will not be long before they break into their set and start the party for real. Rod recognizes this and fumbles around his bed some more. Eventually, he produces a small plastic bag containing a white sheet of paper covered in a series of identical dolphin pictures.

"Want to dose?" he asks, knowing full well what the response will be.

"What you got this week," I question, "dolphins? Just like your shirt. I can see what theme you're on currently."

"Yah, man, this is some seriously sweet stuff. Smoother than those sugar cubes we did last time."

"Smoother, eh? Well, all right then! Lay it on me."

He hands me five small paper squares pinched between the tips of some tweezers. I drop the doses into my mouth, let them sit on my tongue for a second or two, and then swallow them down. The sensation of swallowing them always produces a funky pinching sensation in my chest, despite the fact that I will not feel the effects of the acid for about forty-five minutes. I consider for a moment how powerful psychological effects are upon the body. If people keep thinking that they are sick, then they will be eventually. If they believe that they can run a hundred miles, then their bodies will obey the commands that their minds give them. Of course, how they feel afterwards is another case entirely.

"So, how many sets is the band going to play tonight?"

Rod breaks off his stare into nothingness and focuses his pupils on me. They have enlarged to the size of small quarters, rounded brown coins stuck loosely on his face, and in their dullness I wonder what he sees when he looks at me. He coughs briefly and turns his eyes toward some non-descript spot on the carpet.

"Three, I think, but I'm not really sure. It's hard to tell since they lost their drummer."

"Why is it," I laugh, "that it is always the drummer who suffers the bad luck in bands? Why not the singer or lead guitarist?"

"I don't know, man," Rod chuckles back, "but I love that scene in the film when they're talking about all the drummers that they've lost, the one that implodes and the one that chokes to death on someone else's vomit. That shit is fucking hilarious."

"But it goes to eleven," I spout, and the two of us break into spasms of laughter that last until the rolling harmonics of the band's first song break in on us.

"Oop, time to go," Rod says, rolling to his feet.

We open the door onto a busy scene. Scores of hippies have crowded into the open space at the end of the hall, some standing around the edges, against the walls, a few sitting in various places on the floor. Others dance fluid jigs in front of the band's two microphones where Matt and Mark play their Ibanez guitars in joyful abandon. Rod and I take a seat to the right of the band in the land of discarded mattresses; our bodies feel too heavy at present to maintain a vertical stance.

"We're going to stand one day in the promise land," the band intones. "Freedom! Freedom!"

Numerous cheers and clapping accompany the two long-haired blondes as they guide the crowd through a musical festival of hippy dreams and aspirations. All around the room an excited and ecstatic energy flows between the people. One can feel it flowing in a continuous line from body to body. Here, now, we are all one. We are friends and partners, and the music acts as the glue binding us together.

From out of the hallway, Krystal glides into the center of the room, nude as usual. She has a way of making an entrance and captivating the crowd. Her body glistens with sweat and metallic sparkles, and curvy azure paint circles around her eyes and coats her lips and nipples. The erotic, yet natural, display of her naked flesh lifts the group to a new level of arousal. The band escalates the beat, while the dancers jump about in a more frenetic manner.

In the center of it all, Krystal gyrates like some serpentine goddess.

Time as a concept begins to dissipate from the room. One can believe that we have been fully moved out of the common universe and settled into the expansive void of eternity. Right here, right now, this pleasure is all that matters. Outside of this room, nothing else exists or has any importance. Events start to fly by like the fast forwarding of a video cartridge, and nothing stands out with particular clarity.

Jean-Paul Corriveau

The only aspect of this part of the party that one might be able to recall will be the continuous stream of music that ties the events together.

I watch passively while Krystal becomes tired of dancing and approaches us with a lit candle to talk and relax.

I lie back unconcerned as random people enter and exit the room.

I even get up to dance during one short segment of the set without fully understanding what force helps me to move the limbs of my body.

All these occurrences happen while I seem to watch from deep within my body.

At some point, the band decides to break for a bit and sets their guitars against the boxes of loose equipment stacked along the main wall. Many people file out of the room to head upstairs into the cooler climate of the kitchen and living room, and the ones who stay light up a large number of candles for purpose of mood. Someone across the room pats against his conga drum for a few minutes before breaking into a rhythmic beat. His playing acts as a catalyst for a number of others who pick up nearby bongos and congas and overlap his rhythm with their own. One unique fellow to my right holds up the end of what appears to be a log stripped of bark, and he blows into it to create a deep resonate hum that underscores the plethora of percussive patterns. The effect of this tribal orchestra is to vibrate loose a person's sense of self from the mundane. It has a strangely spiritual influence, and I personally begin to feel my mind rise up from the morass of my body to slowly diffuse into the essence of existence. It is wonderful.

A cold, wet sensation snaps me back into my body. My gaze rolls down to find a straw colored dog pushing his nose against my elbow. I lift my lead filled hand and carefully stroke him on the rounded part of his head between his pyramidal ears. As I do, he sits up on his front paws to converse with me.

"This is the life, isn't it, pal? No worries. No fuss. Just get to lie back and enjoy the scenery. Yeah."

I stare at him with a slightly incredulous, but deeply intrigued expression on my face. The dog seems to take no notice.

"So," he barks, "how did that girl taste earlier, huh? Salty, I bet, yeah. Salty. That's the best isn't it? Yeah, a real slice of life. Do you think you want to stay a wolf?"

I get no chance to reply because the dog's master pats the floor and summons him back across the room. The two of them wrestle playfully. I look at Rod, but he seems to be unaware that I had just been talking with someone's pet. I continue to sit there wondering if what I think just happened did actually just happen, but I am not able to arrive at a conclusion. That seems to be the problem with trying to understand one's own trip by oneself; many outside occurrences cannot be adequately explained. To quote a line from one of Rod and my earlier acid sessions during our college days, "we have to argue to maintain a constant reality."

Across the room, the Native American solemnly materializes in the middle of three of the conga players. The drummers do not realize that he stands among them, and they continue to slap their palms against the stretched yellowish skins of the drums without pause. The Native American does not attempt to talk. He simply stands there watching me with a serious demeanor. He does not bear the look of sadness or frustration that he had earlier in my car or at Violet's house, and he seems to want me to realize something that he will not speak aloud. I think about all the little paternal lectures he has given me over the past year. Then it hits me. He mentioned a vision quest that the men of his tribe engaged in for spiritual purposes. It involved the use of natural, psychoactive drugs and was a major turning point in a young brave's life. Does he wish for me to embark on a vision quest? Is that what he meant in the car about my improper use of the sacred plants? I think it is, but how would I start a vision quest, anyway?

Without my realizing it, my mind drifts off. I find myself imagining some bare-chested ancestor of the Native American's striding confidently through the forest toward some pre-prepared cave that has been set aside for this specific ritual. The warrior breaks into a run as I watch, and as he weaves through the undergrowth my disembodied eyes fall in behind him to follow his paths as he moves. Little by little, my sight pulls in closer to his body. Soon, I find myself fusing into his flesh. I have moved inside the scene. I live it.

There is no questioning why this has occurred. It simply has.

The two of us, in one form, run through the trees and bask in the delight of our body's movements. It is a refreshing sensation. Before long, our essences become so closely joined that we are like one soul. I forget about myself at the party, and he forgets about the formalities of his impending vision quest. We just continue running under the warm sun and through the maternal foliage, enjoying our being, in and of itself.

The land rises up a short distance ahead to form an unusual bow shaped mountain. In the shadow of the curve, I can see the stone dwellings of a Mesa Verde type village carved against the rock face. The place seems uninhabited and ruined, but I feel a pull in that direction just the same. Oddly, my body zips past the village, just as I reach it. I find myself scaling the cliff face, pushing my body toward some further destination, the one that had actually been calling me. I can sense it above me in the clouds. The cliff face changes into a tree-covered slope, but I scramble onward. My thoughts are focused completely upon my goal. Then, abruptly, I am upon it, a golden-lit glade, centered directly upon the flat top of the hill. Sunlight streams down into the area angled bars, and the light breeze caresses the tall grass in musical fashion. A clear, fresh-watered pond invites me to drink from its seat in the middle of the glade. This is paradise, I think, and turn my face to the comforting sky with bright eyes.

Suddenly, an unexpected pang grips my abdomen. I glance about to determine the cause, and I see a bumpy green lizard lying on a nearby branch. One of its large, lidless eyes stares deep into my soul sending a trickle of ice water sliding down my spine. I shiver uncontrollably. What is this creature doing in my Eden? Other inconsistencies that I had overlooked, earlier, start to spring into my vision. Cobwebs menace me from the spaces between the tree trunks; the white sacks of entangled prey hanging casually for the world to see. I had thought them to be dewdrops when I first entered, but now I can see them for what they truly are. Looking down, I see large, undulating worms squirm in the dirt beneath my feet, seeking whatever they consider sustenance. The mutilated forms of their companions are splattered across the underside of my moccasins, and the clay and dirt of the landscape covers my shins and ankles in a mixture of mud and fine powder. I realize that all my skin is covered in muck and sweat and cobwebs. A thin stream of blood rushes over the curves of my face and falls onto my chest, a result of having scrambled through thorns. I am filthy.

"This is not Paradise," I scream. I raise my fist to the heavens. No Eden exists, I think. All such proposed places are built on the shit of the universe. This was never told to us. What we consider good can only be brought about by the toil of slaves. Someone or something must always pay the price for our pleasure, and nothing can exist without first having an opposite.

Rod clasps my arm and shakes me back to the present. "It's okay, man. We are not arguing here. I agree with you. But let's not get into a deep philosophical discussion just yet. Alright?"

"Yeah," I mumble, recognizing that I am in the final bouts of stage one of my dosing.

Rod shifts his body in order to rise into a standing position.

Across the room, the Native American bobs his head approvingly. He raises his palm in farewell and fades from view.

"Wow," I breathe, "I always seem to take off like a rocket every time I do 'cid."

Rod ignores my comment, or fails to hear it. He ambles down the hallway from the now quiet and mostly empty band room. I scrape myself up off the floor and slowly follow after him. I am hungry once again and also desperately thirsty. I catch up with Rod in the kitchen where Krystal is standing naked in front of the stove making Blissballs. "What timing," I laugh to myself. Rod pours us two cups of mystic blue coolade much to my delight. The drink itself is practically luminous due to its intense blue color, and the taste reminds me of the star spangled banner ice pops we used to buy from the ice-cream man as children. I gulp down half of my cup right away before Rod and I sit down upon two of the bar stools that line the kitchen counter. We watch, silently, as Krystal rolls the peanut butter into small balls and drops them into a bowl of poppy seeds. When the poppy seeds cover the entire surface of the balls, she removes them and sets them on a white porcelain plate. Rod and I each grab a ball from the plate and play with it between our fingers before eating. The sensation of squishing the gooey substance in our hands and feeling the peanut butter stick to our skin is too pleasurable to resist. I especially enjoy sucking up the various clumps that I cannot lick off with my tongue. It appears to my drug induced, multi-faceted bug vision that I am picking off shredded pieces of my own flesh. Fortunately, I am not like most and horrified by such sights. If that were the case, I would probably be shrieking in fright like the poor girl a couple of years ago that thought she was eating her own hand instead of a slice of pizza. We had an amazingly difficult time calming her down. I think she has yet to realize that it was only pizza, which proves that some people should never ingest recreational chemicals. It is only for the strong of will and emotion.

In the meantime, Krystal has started cleaning her hands in the sink. I watch as her breasts heave and fall along with the scrubbing motion, and the bright blue paint on her nipples sucks in my attention. The aureoles form tracers in the air as she moves and look like the swirl of a hundred or more sapphire protuberances. I glance back at the neon blue of my drink and then return my gaze to the celestial blue of her painted breasts, and for a second, I contemplate pouring the drink down her bare chest for comparison. The thought never gels into action because I am not in enough control of my muscles to move properly, and this is good since it would have been rude of me to have given her a bath in sugar water without asking. Krystal finishes her cleansing and stalks off out of the kitchen in search of other amusements.

I decide to eat a couple more Blissballs, and this time I savor the flavor. To my right, Rod slowly pages through a notebook that someone had left on the counter. I notice a black ink pen lying near my elbow, and I pick it up and ask Rod for a sheet of paper. Since my vision earlier, I have been thinking about something that I want to save in print for later. Of course, I could not remember to find something to write it with until this moment. My hand quivers from the effects of the acid, and it forces me to grip the pen harder than usual in order to write.

> Thousands of infinite pathways crisscross between the lattices of trees. they form a grid that expands to the limits of my mind. I want to traverse them all, follow each to its own logical conclusion...even though that is impossible. A green haven exists at the end of each path. It is a rising promontory to the heavens, multi-foliate, mounds of earth...

The letters of my words warp and slither about on the page. I have trouble focusing on the lines, and it is with extreme deliberation that I ink every letter. I realize that the hallucinations of stage two have started, in fact had been happening for some time. I force myself to concentrate and finish the paragraph.

> Great spirit, I am sputtering now, save me, I cannot write. Get me back to the pathways…I am stuck on an aerie rooftop being battered by the ferocious wings of Larks' Tongues in Aspic. I want to be everywhere at once. Both inside everything, yet covering everything. I want to let my skin ooze like plasma out over the landscape, cover the environment with my being, then sink down towards the center of the earth, immersing myself amidst every atom, every cell, every fiber of the universe.

The condition gets to be more than I can handle currently. I have to stop. Around me, the entire room starts shifting and changing in dreamlike patterns: the shadows on the walls slide forward and recede similar to waves at a beach; the light from the ceiling bulb transmutes into a tangible substance and whips about the room like a DNA spiral, or perhaps like taffy in a centrifuge. Underneath the bar stools, the speckled linoleum floor disappears and leaves a cloudy yellow atmosphere. I find myself floating high above a gaseous planet. I am an inconsequential speck staring down upon an alien world, entranced by the sight I see. Flying lizards with slow flapping bat wings pass by, and hovering crystals in the shape of professionally cut diamonds form a path to the horizon. About me, the clouds that constitute the body of this planet continue to swirl in strange non-symmetrical patterns. I find myself awed by the beauty of this view.

"Come on, man," Rod beckons, acting once again as my eternal reminder of an agreed upon reality. "Let's go into the back yard and listen to some King Crimson and stare at the night sky."

"Rod," I want to say. "You just wrenched me back from the farther dimensions by my silver cord. Why must you always ground me in the here and now?" I think about our observation again—we have to argue to maintain a constant reality. That seems to become more and more applicable as the moments, I mean days, I mean, I don't know what, pass. Who knows what plane I would be traipsing across if I were physically alone?

The grass of the backyard feels cool upon my back and legs as we lie down next to a trio of guys I do not recognize. They shift their bodies uncomfortably to signal that our intrusion has interrupted their peace of mind. We ignore them and gaze up towards the stars that appear so close we should be able to reach out and touch them. I try grabbing one out of sheer orneriness to see if the feat is possible. My hand glows silver from the stardust. To the northwest, the moon has risen high above the mountain peaks, and its face is a perfectly rounded hole in the sky allowing the light of creation to shine through. "That is me up there," I tell myself as I slip into the third stage of my trip. I am the hole that exposes the light behind the veil. I am the revealer of existence. The moon is not a woman like the Greeks and Christians believe. The moon is male. Like the Native Americans believe. I am the moon. I share its changes, its growth, and decline. I mostly come out at night—when all is silent and calm.

One of the guys turns to his companion and whispers a question. "Did you know that it takes the light from one of those stars a hundred or so years to reach us?"

"Yeah, man," replies his friend. "Wouldn't it be cool if we saw one of them suddenly go out?"

I laugh loudly, breaking up the serenity of the moment. Rod and the other three glance over in fearful agitation. They want me to stop before their drug created paranoia becomes too much. I keep laughing until the tears race down my face.

"Wouldn't it be cool," I gasp between chuckles. "Wouldn't it be cool if we saw them all suddenly disappear?"

Their eyes grow large and white in the darkness. My laughter surrounds them.

I feel sated now. There is nothing to do but rest my head upon the skulls of my victims. Out in the darkness I can hear the sheep gathering close together in the valley in a pathetic attempt to stave off their fear. Why do they not realize that we should only be afraid of ourselves? I lick the last of the blood from my whiskers and sigh. I may rest, now, but tonight will not prove enough.

Tomorrow I must embark on the hunt again.

Part 2: Dark Portraits

"Elle est retrouvee! Quoi? L'eternite.
C'est la mer melee au soleil.
Mon ame eternelle, Observe ton voeu
Malgre la nuit seule Et le jour en feu.
Donc tu te degages Des humains suffrages, Des communs élans!
Tu voles selon…
—Jamai l'esperance. Pas d'orietur.
Science et patience, Le supplice est sur.
Plus de lendemain, Braises de satin, Votre ardeur Est le Devoir."
-Rimbaud

For some,

The night acts as a haven. The tender arms of shadow curl comfortingly about one's body and bring a sense of energy as well as solace. The evening breeze carries the exotic scent of distant lands, and the haze of street lamps and building lights suggests the possibility of other worlds hiding beneath the surface of accepted reality. Even the humming sounds of far away cars and the sharp explosion of the occasional voice echoing from some twisting alley manages to add to a delicious sense of the mystery in life. One cannot help but realize that there exists some unknown force in the universe and that he or she is not exactly alone when walking the streets after the sun has set.

The night then, when objectively examined, represents the dark, unexplained possibilities of life. Flights of the soul, yearning for knowledge, projection of desire— these all take place under the protective auspices of the midnight realm. Shadows reign in this netherworld where doorways quietly open onto other planes of existence and creatures stealthily prowl the dim walkways between dimensions. The denizens of this realm are explorers and visionaries by choice. They travel along the corridors of experience and boldly walk through gateways to the future. They search for truth in Being.

On one street named Broadway in the edge city called Denver, a handful of these particular denizens gather regularly at weekend to communally express their nocturnal allegiance. They arrive silently, emerging from the palpable darkness of side roads and walkways to take their place in line outside the rusting metal door of a non-descript, brown building situated along a block of storefronts and businesses near the heart of town. The façade of the building presents little unusual to the casual observer. Nothing suggests that this locale acts as a Nexus for bringing together those beings who stride under the sable moon. Nothing reveals its designated purpose.

One focal being in the group attracts particular notice. He is the Nameless One. His lithe body rises at least half a foot higher than most of the others standing about him, and his fine features and pale skin seem to glow like white fire beneath the deep black of his accoutrements. He stands calmly about two thirds of the way back in a line that winds northward along the sidewalk, and he has pushed his hands into the pockets of his thick black leather pants. Despite the fact that he only wears a thin nylon and lycra shirt upon his upper torso, he seems oblivious to the chill, swirling air. The Nameless One simply gazes at the black vinyl and lace wearing men and women about him and thinks to himself that this brood could be considered his young. These ebony clad beings are his children, and they represent the current generation of the so-called Goth lineage.

The regulars in the crowd are easiest to spot. Cynthia Dekoevend, for example, the strong-featured Nordic beauty, stands arrogantly toward the front of the line, her six-foot height making her a quick mark. She has henna laced, auburn hair this week, a nice shift to something subtle after the glaring yellows and blues and purples she has sported at previous gatherings, and it complements the fake jaguar skin, body-length coat she flaunts. Her high-heeled stiletto boots are the sole objects protruding from underneath the coat, and they alone offer little in assisting the viewer to determine the nature of the outfit she has concealed—not that it matters what Cynthia wears at any one time. She is an elder, and her attitude expresses her power and passion.

The same cannot be said for the German as he fidgets about four people back from Cynthia. As usual, he wears the black vinyl pants and black fishnet tank top that has perpetually adorned his frame at previous gatherings. He rarely changes the combination or adds to it, believing that these specific items most effectively draw attention to his shaved muscular torso, his bulging biceps, solid pectorals, and washboard stomach. He does not pause to consider that wearing the same clothes, gathering after gathering, only bores the people whose attention he hopes to obtain. He actually assumes it is a compliment when he hears the others mention how gauche he appears as he passes by them.

Toward the back of the line, Vernon, the acolyte, paces eagerly. The excitement of being part of a gathering shows plainly on his face, and his eagerness to join the festivities is as apparent as the black Utchat he has painstakingly inscribed about his right eye. For him, the symbol is merely an end to his stage of initiation. He considers it to be nothing more than a physical sign that he has become worthy to join the exalted ones and that he has advanced to a stage that can be considered truly alternative in nature. Vernon does not realize that a greater power lies behind the symbol, nor

My dear feline,

I hope everything goes darkly with you. I hope that your journey has proven exciting and worthwhile. Your last communiqué leads me to assume that this is so, but sadly I cannot reply the same concerning my own path. The path I travel seems dim of late because I have been walking through the barren lands of the mundane world. I find this place repulsive. The people here remain so bloated and ignorant, so drab and colorless, and not one of them betrays a spark of life. Why do we subsist on them? Their bodies and minds are weak, they seem completely unable to grasp even the most basic tenants within philosophical, cosmological, and ontological arguments, and they mill about like bovines wasting their brief moments of existence waiting for the slaughter. Pardon the expression, but they are "as dumb as doorknobs". At this point in my travels across the universe, I have come to the conclusion that the origin of this mental and physical indolence in our culture lies within the fact that the average, mundane person actually believes in the labels and categories that society attempts to assign to the objects about us. The average, mundane, in other words, refuses to step beyond the system's created illusions to see the truth underneath. As a result, these people continue to plod through time like automatons granted a smidgeon of emotion, and while the system tells them what to think and feel and provides them with comfort and ease they blindly follow along with its inhuman drive.

Let me provide you with an example that I feel exposes the illusions woven by corporate America in order for it to maintain docility, productivity, and banality within its subjects. I know that the previous paragraph causes me to sound like something of a raving liberal, which I detest, and I know that you will not simply take me on my word so here is a situation for you to dwell upon. An inspirational quote had been distributed around what will remain an undisclosed company, during a rather trying period when most of the workers were being pressed into mandatory, unpaid, overtime. The fragmented quote simply said, "one day I know that I will reach the end of this long road". Now, since this was a quote, presumably from some authoritative and common personage (as far as the workers knew), and since it had been released in the specific context of an increased, compulsory workload, the workers readily took the statement to mean that their hard work would prove worthwhile some unspecified time in the future when they would find the peace and relaxation they deserve from being so productive, such as retirement, holiday, or even shorter hours. The workers automatically believed in the supposedly undisputable truth of this previously arranged interpretation (that is, an interpretation forced upon them, not open to them), and they acted exactly as the company hoped they would by sacrificing more time out of their already overburdened existence in order to meet its arbitrary, capitalistic needs. These workers unquestioningly accepted the company's doctrine and psychic manipulation, and, to put it more simply, the workers allowed the company to impose a rigid template for living upon their own mental schemata. Had any one of these workers taken the time to research the quote that had been spoon fed to them, he or she would have learned that the person who had written the quote was a poet, not a commoner. He or she would also have realized that the original intention behind the quote was to instill a lust for life in the reader, in the hopes that the reader would attempt to experience more of the splendor of existence. The long road mentioned in the quote was meant to be a metaphor for life, itself, and the end of the road represented death. The writer's true intent had been to get the reader to consider that one day he or she would pass from this world into the great unknown. This would not be does he even grasp the origin of its design. The ancient, body glyph will not be activated by this traveler, even should he be made privy to its capabilities, and it will never reveal to him the secrets that the faith's ancient adherents manage to unearth. Vernon has never been true blood, and because of this his position among the Nocturnals will remain offensively static as the nights fade into each other.

Beltram, lastly, happens to be the only other regular to have arrived before the opening. He leans against the brick wall of the building, striking a match against the silver metal zipper of his biker jacket before using it to light a Marlboro. As the tip attains a fiery, crimson, glow, he takes a couple drags from the butt and then absently pulls the cigarette out of his mouth to allow for his casual exhale. The smoke curls into indecipherable patterns while he lets his fingers stroke at the rectangular goatee jutting out from the base of his chin. About both sides of his face, the hair cascades down onto his chest like twin coal-colored waterfalls. He appears every bit the powerful pharaoh garbed in modern day leather. For some reason, known only to him, Beltram has come alone. He stands aloof of the others and stares out at the surrounding attendees with hard snake-slit eyes. Beltram holds rank as part of one of the original dynasties of Nocturnal elders. His age and experience make him a dangerous individual to know, and the younger, newer gatherers naturally gravitate away from him out of fear and respect. They can sense the disdain he has for their posturing.

A loud thock echoes out into the street as the bolt is thrown from behind the entrance to the building. The door opens outward and exposes a hired ghoul and a passageway into the building's depths. Those in line quickly file into the newly formed aperture and find themselves crossing over into a vast open hall, where most of them, including the Nameless One and the elders, immediately head toward one of the two descending staircases on the room's far side. The staircases plunge down into the earth along barren cement tunnels and dank stone passages and end at the open maws of a subterranean crypt. Above the entrances to this underworld domain, broken wooden plaques hang and proclaim this place "The Wreck Room"

In prior years, tradition required that a Nocturnal be announced upon entering a gathering's event chamber. The Master of Ceremonies would wait patiently by the arch entranceway and would shout in a loud tone the name of the personage immediately arriving; the reasoning for this being that Nocturnals did not exist in great numbers and that the importance of recognizing each other by face and nom d'emprunt was tantamount to survival in those days. The gatherings then proceeded like meetings of state where debates on the floor ensued over a plethora of issues. The elder Nocturnals wandered from group to group engaging in constant conversation, and they made the point of garnering a consensus as to how Nocturnals could prolong and protect their existence among the sun worshippers. This consensus was then an option. As the writer saw it, life was short, and every moment needed to be embraced and cherished. No one should waste time performing drudging labor for someone else's benefit. Had the workers actually spent some time to examine this quote and consider it in depth, in context with the entire poem, they probably would have become cognizant of the fact that the company had completely reversed the meaning of the quote and deliberately transformed it into a frighteningly repressive platitude. The workers would then have managed to punch a small hole through the wall of illusion established by the system, and for the first time grown beyond the limits imposed by society. Unfortunately, in this case, no one employee seemed able to pierce the veil of lies spread by the corporation. Each worker dutifully fulfilled the required overtime with little or no afterthought.

So, I offer the following morsel. "A bad spirit drieth the bones". Growl it out loud. "A BAD SPIRIT DRIETH THE BONES". Do you like the poetic nature of the line? The casual iambic pentameter? You will never guess what book contains this passage. No, not in a millennium. Have any luck yet? Yes? No? Hmmmmmm. Need a hint? Well, too bad. Maybe someday I will enlighten you if you remain unable to discover the source. Anyhow, I mention this now because I feel that it happens to be a rather apropos line considering my last paragraph. I feel that the established systems controlling human development are the evil spirit warned against in that passage. They are legion...ha, ha, ha. They create a world of illusions in order to enslave the human race. Of course, I also feel that you have already recognized this fact. That happens to be why you and I exist as a breed apart from the common mundane. We are strong, we are beautiful, and we determine our own course through existence. We do not accept any singular interpretation of anything unless it comes from our own firsthand knowledge, and often not even then. We are not the submissive bags of carbon that the rest of the race allow themselves to be. I will quote from one of our kind this time, that being the man who is Andrew Eldritch, to emphasize this point. He sings, "we look hard...we look through". Self-induced blindness to universal injustice will never be our kind's style. We will always live to reveal the truths beneath the surface, and we will always ride the storm. Were our literary progenitor, Hamlet, to live today, he might analyze our kind in much the self-same fashion. Like us, he alone was willing to confront the corruption rampant within the system. For him, it was government-sponsored murder. For us, it is mental genocide.

To step off on a tangent, do you know that the other day, a most amazing and in some manner terrifying mutation occurred in me. My eyes turned hourglass. As I strolled along a city street, all objects began to wither and melt inside my field of vision. A young girl, exuberant and sassy, shriveled up in rapid succession as I watched; her vibrant hair turned gray and stringy, while the liquid beneath her flesh seemed to evaporate right through the pores. Her skin grew brown and taut as she drew close, the substance stretching with age, until it became so brittle that the dermal layers could not withstand the pressure. They tore violently. Some invisible force then physically pulled the tattered flesh and muscle from her face, so that only the ivory skull with its hollow sockets remained. I stood there stunned. This was alarming. Similarly, I noticed that all the flowers along the walkways began to lose their petals and decay. The petals fell off in slow motion, one by one, and as each individual fan-shaped bud dropped to the ground a severe black rot engulfed it completely. Even buildings and statues crumbled before me, their granite and marble frames billowing into hazy dust within moments of my glancing at them. It appeared that everything I turned inked in hieroglyph on papyrus and read aloud to the assembled crowd before the revelries would begin. That was then.

These nights, Nocturnals co-exist somewhat with their daytime counterparts, yea even flourish, providing they do not extensively dispel the façade of normalcy established by the mundane sun worshippers. Nocturnals exist in droves in this decade and because of this permitted leisure the formalities of the ancient codes have either been forgotten or diluted in contemporary bastardizations of communal exercise. The new generation feels no need to worry about survival or collaboration. They casually stroll into the chamber proper, take their accustomed places with little or no acknowledgement from their peers, and prepare for an evening of hedonism and escapism as opposed to academic conversation. If they open up discussion these nights, the subjects are mostly cosmetic, covering such topics as fashion or the current drug of choice. Even the Master of Ceremonies has faded into the background. He hides himself behind the impersonal barrier of a mixing board, turntables, and sound system, and his voice becomes the emotion producing vibrations of recorded music and digital manipulation.

Tonight, the Master of Ceremonies chooses a creepy organ sound to accompany the evening's gatherers and invoke a Halloween style mood in them as they slide into the underground chamber. The sound projects from numerous speakers hung in strategic locations about the ceiling, and it covers the breadth of the room like a supernatural presence. Rows of purple fluorescent black lights add to the sinister ambience and transform the incoming Nocturnals into shadow blackened wraiths or for those in white garments angelic glowing entities. These creatures mill about aimlessly and create the effect that one has entered into a replica of the judgement grounds of Anubis.

The Nameless One squats down within the shadow of a wide column that is one of many supporting the ceiling. He remains still, the emotionless expression upon his face betraying nothing of his inner thoughts. Only his eyes shift as Cynthia Dekoevend strolls by without her jaguar coat. She has removed her outerwear to reveal a striking dominatrix outfit replete with fishnet stockings above the aforementioned stiletto boots, tight black underwear curving gracefully in all the right places, long ballroom gloves stretching past her elbows, and of course the personally fitted corset top reinforced with straps and glinting silver metal rings. Wrapped around her neck is a silver spiked dog collar. She ignores the stares of some of the younger attendees and coolly heads toward the front of the dance floor where the M.C.'s box sits. The German cranes his neck to watch her progress. He feels outdone yet again, but he remains determined to make an impression. Determinedly, he grabs a pair of fingerless, leather gloves from his pocket and pulls them over his hands in a superficial way of *my attention upon suddenly revealed its impermanence within eternity. I must admit that I found myself struck sober by the raw profundity of this vision. Since then, I have found myself powerless to escape these sights when they occur. There have been moments when I have been conversing with another person, and their face abruptly falls to the floor leaving nothing but chattering bone and darkened pits. I ask, "has this ever happened to you?"*

No, do not answer that question. I wish to move on to another subject. I was reading Camus the other day when I vividly recalled a childhood experience stored deep within my mind. One second, I was visualizing the seedy bar in Amsterdam described by Camus' rich prose, and the next I was propelled back to my parents' house in Texas to a time that existed shortly after the birth of my brother. Like in most children's rooms, my bed had been set in the far corner across from the dresser and box of toys. The edge of the bed had not been entirely pushed against the wall, and it left approximately a foot of space open on that side. I can remember no reason for this. The memory shifted abruptly to a visual angle where I found myself staring up at the ceiling. I understood, inherently, that I was now lying upon a beanbag across the top of my bed and that I was rolling slightly from side to side. The force of one roll brought me to the edge of the bed. I nearly tumbled off, and I experienced a shocking sense of vertigo that zipped through my entire body. My youthful reflexes allowed me to adjust quickly by rolling back in the opposite direction and returning myself to the center of the bed and stability, but as my breathing slowed to a normal rate, I realized that I had become rather excited by the near cataclysmic event. I wanted to feel that rush again. With impish delight, I began to rock myself back and forth again in the hopes of bringing myself back to that dramatic moment of looming over the edge. It did not take long to occur. As I tipped toward the chasm below, time seemed to freeze and position me within a temporal stasis. I heard my mind telling me that I had a decision to make. I could pull back now and return to the support of the center of the bed, or I could allow myself to continue on my present course and plunge to the bottom of the abyss. The choice had to be made at that very moment. Here I was, hardly four years of age, and I had such a weighty matter to ponder. I chose to fall, of course, and the drop lasted far longer than my childish mind could comprehend. It did not matter. The fall was pure ecstasy, a deliciously slow spinning sensation that removed my mind from the dull dregs of another empty day. I could hardly recall landing, the sensation remained with me for such a lengthy period of time. I just vaguely remembered the disappointment at having arrived at the end of the trip. Immediately, I proposed to myself that I would return to the pinnacle of my bed so that I could repeat the fall once more. That determination had subconsciously been the whole of my recollection until now.

Doubtless, you would say that I have been over-influenced by my reading material. That may, perhaps, be true, but the validity of the memory cannot be disputed. If my evening studies have had any effect upon my mind in this situation, it has been merely to conjure up a deeply rooted memory that has been lying dormant until now, not create a past scenario outright.

But, I know, you always prefer to dwell in the present. I suppose, therefore, that you would like me to discuss the more current events in my life. I have no qualm with that. I have recently been spending a greater amount of my weekend nights at a little club entitled "1082". The atmosphere is rather enjoyable. Dark. Moody. Industrial. The DJ utilizes an excellent selection of discs when mixing each night. I have known only a handful of places that have had the true underground grit to spin such (r)evolutionary bands augmenting his normal dress code. He strokes his ego and tells himself that he has made a gigantic stride forward.

The music shifts then into a faster, electronic song. The M.C. has put on some early eighties industrial, specifically the hardcore dance beats of Nitzer Ebb. Suddenly, the air feels buffeted by the winds fanned off the wings of demons, and the floor vibrates in imitation of the treading of the gods. A group of topless males, their bodies adorned in an array of colorful tattoos leap out onto the floor and begin dancing in jerky motions. Lances of purple light fly off of the shiny metal piercings in their noses and lips and ears and nipples, in all directions, and their energy infuses the other gatherers and imbues the whole area with a new life. A few of the new children decide to join the body artists on the dance floor, while the music gradually moves into a classic Skinny Puppy song. Slowly, more gatherers arrive through the two-stepped entranceways from the upper world. From his position under the concrete column, the Nameless One grins broadly.

It is but a short while later that the Divine Twins make their stunning appearance. A mysterious pair of females, these two elders never speak to another soul, and no one, not even the Nameless One, have been able to determine if they are truly sisters or are lovers, instead. Per usual, they stride into the chamber arm in arm with the confident swagger of dominant personalities. This week, both have on flashy metallic outfits—one gold in color, the other silver. The outfits consist of form-fitting mini-skirts that barely pass the lower curve of their derrières, strapless tube-tops that allow their nipples to poke through the sheer material, high-heeled clogs, and enticingly enough, wigs to match the color of their shiny garments. Their arrival absorbs the attention of every attendee in the room, and the two make a glittery, sensual procession to their favorite spot at the front of the dance floor, a single pole that the two love to writhe and slink about in the manner of professional strippers. Immediately, they begin their performance for the night.

The Nameless One rises to a standing position. He spreads out his arms in the form of a devotee welcoming Ra's face at dawn, and he basks in the pleasure of feeling his body move. He has grown weary of the opening festivities, where personal style is paraded around as if the gatherers are on a stage. He ponders avoiding the opening from this point forward. His equal in generation, Beltram, always disappears during the beginning moments to pursue the gods know what fiendish endeavors, and the Nameless One debates whether he should likewise retire himself to some hidden alcove. The thought seems tempting, yet the Nameless One realizes that the glamour and flash of the exhibitions actually entertain him somewhat. The keep him connected on a superficial level to the younger crowd. He may feel discouraged by the pomp at this current moment, but he knows that this will not always be the case. Without the posturing of the younger ones to watch, he would feel less energized as Thrill Kill Kult and the Legendary Pink Dots. Our kind needs more havens like this one. We deserve more places to unwind. Many of the attendees, unfortunately, disturb my sensibilities. I detect a more care-free and violent current in the personalities of this younger generation, and their tendencies toward posturing are disproportionately large. They place a greater emphasis on fashion and style than on experience and knowledge. Fashion and style have their place as a means of expressing one's internal makeup, but to judge another solely upon their choice of accoutrements is (I have to speak it) to fall into the mundane fallacy of stereotyping. That is not haute couture, as I know it. And the recreational use of chemicals in that group has no spiritual aspect to it. No social aspect, either, from what I can tell. Their consumption of psychoactive materials tends to fall into one or two of the following categories—addiction, rebellious spite, or escapism. What happened to the endeavor to elevate oneself to a higher state of consciousness? Where is the desire to ascend out of this state of shite that the deadmen allow to perpetuate around us? Lasciate ogne speranza, voi ch'intrate. I, personally, will not be crushed under the weight of the horde. The younger brood appears not to care, though. They revel in irresponsibility and libidinous recklessness. Were we the same at that point? Not quite, I say. Being inexperienced may be one thing, but to let loose the beast with such abandon seems another. You might play devil's advocate, throw up a rebuttal, and say that I have begun to grow out of touch with the current age, which would be true to a certain extent, but I know that this self-destructiveness in their nature exists at a much more dangerous level than for previous broods. Our outpouring of angst and frustration and sexuality found root in art and increased experience. The dissatisfaction in our lives led towards a metamorphosis into homo superior, not towards the destruction of our lives and others. What has happened to creation over time? I recall a much different progression toward Nirvana and have to ask, "where have all the golden ones gone?" "There were giants in the earth in those days." I interject here another quote from the source that I am sure you have not determined, yet. But I digress. Believe me, this streak of viciousness needs to be addressed quickly. I fear that if we do not take action, the horde will grow ever larger, and all that we have achieved so far will be lost. Do I hear the toll of the cathedral bell? Let us look to our children and guide them lest we become as the Morlocks.

Yes. I recognize that attitude of yours. That arched brow suggests that I have gotten overly polemic. Not to worry. I have less serious subjects to discuss from here on out. As much as I believe you should consciously deliberate on what I have argued so far, I will not end this missive on an academic note.

A few weeks ago, I met a delicious specimen of female. She was a walking Rodin sculpture with her arms gracefully swaying beside her body in serpentine elegance and her head fixed in regal poise. I felt truly captivated by the glamour, and her every breath whispered of power and passion. As she strolled by, our glances connected. Staring into her eyes reminded me of diving into a crystalline pool. She stopped in mid-stride and settled her hands on her hips; the defiance made readily apparent as we spent a number of moments analyzing each other's inner being. I recognized the mark upon her, the blazing crimson that only our kind can intuit. She obviously sensed it in me as well because she dropped the mask of intimidation and stepped up close. I detected the scent of ancient evenings upon her skin. Had we been somewhere less public, I would have ravaged her right there, but instead the two of us agreed to retire to a secluded spot where we could engage in the Ritual of Acknowledgement. The conversation had been scintillating, as they say. The topics ranged from Jung to Crowley to Barker to Latrec, and before I realized the time, the waking sun had than he does at present, so he ejects the thoughts from his mind and walks toward one darkened corner to where a group of young ones are partaking of the drug, Ecstasy. He procures a dose from a short Latino youth whose face is like a cherub. The seductive glance given by the boy cannot be mistaken, and the two agree to retire to one of the cement benches along the side of the chamber and become acquainted.

Lord Abydon rushes into the chamber at this moment. The billows of his black cloak flutter wildly in his wake, and he glances about quickly with eyes surrounded by black paint shaped like bat wings. He looks for Cynthia Dekoevend. As most gatherers understand, the two share a bond, and it has been rumored that his ability to rise to elder was due to his connection with her. But this cannot be argued too loudly in public. Any such Nocturnal decrying this fact at a gathering will find themselves directly chastised by Cynthia herself. She does not appreciate rumors concerning her private affairs, and Lord Abydon has no compunction in showing others that he is immensely grateful for her protection in this matter. His devotion to her is not entirely without substance, though. After a few moments of panicked searching, he sees his amour dancing by the Divine Twins and hurries to bestow his affection with an enthusiastic embrace, not noticing any other creature about him.

The Divine Twins spit disgustedly as he draws close.

The hall is now almost full after nearly an hour and a half. From his booth at the foot of the dance floor, the M.C. begins to play the Marilyn Manson tune, "The Beautiful People", which happens to be a crowd favorite. Scores of individuals and couples flock to the dance floor to join with the rhythm of the music. Their bodies twist and contort and transmute into a variety of animal shapes—the elegant ibis, the regal hawk, the sleek jackal. Most of the gatherers metamorphasize into serpents, their arms curving toward the ceiling like the slender shape of an asp rising from the ground, their hips swaying gently and hypnotically, their feet a solid base. About the floor, the red and yellow spotlights flare to life and drown the eye in bold color. The mood has become more aggressive and intense because of the M.C.'s manipulations of the past couple songs, and his skill has turned the chamber into a Den of Set.

The Nameless One steps onto the dance floor to join with the others. He has left the boy with his ghoul toy back on the bench, and his erratic movements evince his fury. He cannot believe that the boy had the audacity to invite some boorish drunkard into their impromptu coterie. He had been about to suck on the boy's neck when this lumbering mundane fool decided to sit beside them. The stench was enough to knock a god unconscious, and the Nameless One had stood and shot the boy a killing stare, his personal eye of Horus. The boy managed to laugh and throw his arms about the mundane. He was obviously too young to realize the danger he placed himself in by angering an elder. Needless to say he would not be seen at this gathering again.

begun to paint the sky a blotched peach color from its position beneath the horizon. We had to rush back to our respective lairs in order to take our required sleep, though we agreed to continue our bonding session that very night. I barely rested. A vision of her face had become imprinted on my mind, and the thought of her next to my body set my fingertips on fire.

As I crossed her threshold that night, my new companion's domicile gave off the appearance of utilizing a minimalist décor. That initial impression would never leave me, yet the longer I was to stay the more the place conveyed an earthy attitude as well. There were a few bare oak sofas and chairs pushed against the walls, and pale brown cattails sprouted from copper urns in the corners. Square Persian rugs had been thrown across a couple choice areas of the hardwood floor, and a few potted plants hung at different heights from golden, gilded rings twisted into the ceiling. Aside from these Spartan furnishings, three paintings hung upon the walls. They were brightly rendered pieces of abstract expressionism that had risen to popularity forty years ago. They had been framed in polished gold metal and presented in that perfectly arranged, purchased in a yuppy gallery, style. Set in context with the rest of the room, they portrayed my young lady as an amalgamation of simplicity, practicality, and experimentation. Not what I would have conceived earlier considering the slick garments and aggressive personality she exuded on the street. I would have guessed her a Leo, then, but considering the new factors I had to think she landed on the borderline between Capricorn and Aquarius. There was a seeming contradiction floating across this room that defied judgement, and I have to believe that the ambience prepared me for the physical transformation I was about to see in my host.

Meine schone fraulein, stepped out from behind the door with a casual grace. She had pulled her hair back into a pony-tail and donned a pair of small black plastic glasses, the square style that force one to recall the 50's and border on assumed geekiness, while betraying an experienced intelligence. She wore an aged pair of jeans with white patches ready to become holes forming around the knees and under the curves of her derrière, and a white t-shirt hung loosely about her upper torso. She appeared nothing like the urban goddess that I had met the previous evening decked out in leather and lace. She had transformed into a deific cat—beautiful, open, unassuming, and relaxed—and I found myself immediately taken in by this charming aspect of her personality. I grabbed her for an enthusiastic hug to let her know how excited I felt.

The second Ritual of Connection began slowly with the two of us sitting on the couch discussing theological movements. She rose occasionally to make some herbal tea or light a cone of incense, and I settled back into the cushions and let my mind expand. We focused on the pleasant sensation of the words streaming from our mouths like the flow of water down the side of a mountain, and after an hour she shared her inner passion—Wicca. I was delighted but cautious. You might well have guessed this, considering my love of paganism, but I felt a little worried that she might turn out to be one of those flighty, new age gel heads. Fortunately, she proved that her adherence to that particular, alternative system was not strict and that she recognized its limitations. Her studies extended to other occult thinking as well, and she engaged me further by suggesting that we use a number of different divining guides to helps us enhance our bond.

She decided to begin on a fun note and left the room to retrieve a cloth bag of runes from her bedroom. Sadly, I did not fall in tune with these very well. It was the blank rune that naturally gravitated to my hand first, and the rarity of the selection, designated for Odin, himself, made our jaws drop briefly.

Jean-Paul Corriveau

A tall, wispy blonde with her hair pulled into two mane shaped tails along both sides of the back of her head catches the Nameless One's attention. She smiles playfully at him, while simultaneously giving the impression of being demur, but the dark blue shadows encircling both her eyes add to her sultriness and entice him to the fullest extent. In addition, the white half shirt she wears glows under the glare of the black lights just above a bellybutton ring and leads him on more. He licks his lips, stares at the tight leather pants accentuating her thin frame, and glides over to meet her. After the debacle with the Latin youth, he is eager for action and prepared to put the past behind him.

The girl rotates her body in a semi-circle and backs her buttocks up into the Nameless One's erogenous zone. He in turn wraps his arms around her torso and slides his hands underneath her shirt to cup her breasts. The Ecstasy that each of them has taken begins to take effect and arouse them.

About the couple, others start to slip into similar forms of sensuality.

Toward the front of the dance floor, the Divine Twins face each other from different sides of the pole. Their hands clench each other's buttocks, and they slide up and down the pole in sexual simulation while licking each other's tongues. The shortness of their skirts cannot handle the violence of their movements, and this causes the two items to ride up and reveal the ivory smoothness of their behinds and the curly darkness between their legs. Neither seems to care too much about the exposure or their lack of undergarments.

On the three-foot tall block situated between the dance floor and the shadow area filled with tables for drinking and relaxing two couples lie together. The one pair, a couple of lads in t-shirts, skin tight shorts, and large pastel colored boots kiss passionately, their hands slowly roving across each other's body. The second pair, a couple of girls with brown bobbed haircuts and trendy alternative clothes have partially unbuttoned their silk shirts to better enjoy themselves. The taller girl pulls the loosened blouse off of one shoulder of the shorter, Asian girl and licks along her bra strap, then gently bites down in the crevice between her neck and shoulder. The Asian girl moans, lifting her arms up to run her fingers through her Caucasian counterpart's hair.

Sitting at the foot of the dance floor, Cynthia Dekoevend curls her legs and arms around Lord Abydon from behind, pressing him closer to her with a bullwhip. The two calmly watch the activities of the others from their vantage point, knowing full well that their pleasures will come later in the privacy of their own sanctum.

The witching hour has fully settled upon the gathering. Fire and brimstone singe the air, and the atmosphere fairly reeks with the odor of eroticism and sensuality, underscoring the questing nature of contemporary Nocturnals—to strive to attain a heightened sense of self and experience—to push oneself past the limits of mundane existence. That is the key to living in true form. Nocturnal life runs fast

136

Somehow, my companion managed to quickly replace the shock on her face with a smile. I could see, though, that she was internally determining the range of possible meanings that could spring from this culling. I struggled to connect with two more runes, but felt little from the remaining stones. Upon realizing that I would not draw forth another, she nodded knowingly, and a mischievous sparkle blazed in her eye. Her glance betrayed more than most words. I felt positive that she had become captured within the heart of that drawing and that she thought the consequence of its sole connection with myself bore a great importance on the evening. Perhaps, in some small way, that was the truth, but I would not deign to jump to that conclusion as she did. Ra, she was a bold one.

In any case, the incomplete, enticing prophecy left by the runes prompted her to pull out an ornate Tarot deck from a box bearing the great Scarab Seal. She pointed out that the cards had been hand painted by a friend. I was impressed by the design her friend had crafted, and as I watched her lay them out I was not surprised that she opted for the Northern European style of fortune telling and arranged my cards according to the Celtic method. Apparently, she felt she could obtain a better grasp on my existence through this particular type of supernatural opinion. Major Arcana cards dominated the pattern, and I could see that the line up impressed her in turn. She had obviously come to the conclusion that I had a strong position within the Skein. Despite this, only one thing held my attention on the spread—the High Priestess was lying humorously Before Me. There was no subtle way to read this card. I looked up at my companion with a smirk and saw that the reading was definitely not ambiguous. Our eyes met and held, and the nervous embarrassment I found between us caused to me chuckle an evil baritone. Playfully, I queried, "Little Isis?" She breathed out strongly, and her eyes fell towards her knees. When she glanced up again and timidly ran her fingers along my elbow, all the while smiling crookedly, I knew that it was time to act. The energy circled wildly about us, and I drew myself closer to her. We fell into each other's arms for the remainder of the night.

I will not continue to depict the scene as I am a gentleman and a scholar, but I feel confident that you can imagine the elicit details on your own. Instead, I would like to finish my missive by discussing a dream that I had almost forgotten to mention. I believe that this dream might be connected in some way with the visions I described a couple pages ago. Give it a listen and tell me what you think.

The dream begins deep within an infinite void. I am floating helpless, like a child. I say child because this place is like a womb, and I am unconcerned and unmotivated as to learning anything outside of my current situation. Floating feels comfortable and pleasant. I readily accept this absolute state of peace where nothing matters and nothing feels important. I simply want to float and dream my dreams of darkness and serenity, yet, as I hang here, the blackness degenerates into a two-dimensional structure. The space in front of me warps into a thick ebony screen that lacks edges, and onto that screen coalesces a giant skull from out of the nothingness. The skull is terrifying. It is an ancient emblem filled with cracks and sharp, bony curves, and the glare off of its surface pains me. Despite the fact that the skull is bereft of ocular tissue, I cannot shake the sensation that it stares directly into my soul. The scrutiny causes me to feel uneasy and naked, and I want to scream in agony or fly to some remote location where the dark remains warm and undifferentiated and I can forget about this frightening phantom. I desire to feel static again.

and free, and the common rules of morality and suppression do not apply to those who teach the Epicureans to taste.

In the dimly lit section, situated between two ghoul-tended bars toward the back of the chamber, Beltram releases his energy in quite a different manner. He grips Vernon by the neck, having lifted the boy off his feet and pinned him to a wall, and he screams forcibly at the pitiful neonate. Beltram's words are inaudible to the surrounding gatherers, the overwhelming boom of the music easily covers most of the verbal communication in this place, but his anger remains painfully obvious for those who dare to watch.

Beside him, his close confidant, Maabu, the ebony skinned African crosses his immense arms over his chest and exposes the various esoteric symbols that have been branded there. He displays these scars as a testament to his power and laughs at something that Beltram has yelled. Briefly, he shakes a finger at Vernon, like a parent scolding a child, and shakes his bald head in mock disappointment. Those familiar with the relationships between these three Nocturnals know that Vernon has botched another drug transaction for the two elders. His punishment will prove dire indeed.

O Fortuna suddenly blasts across the chamber and whips the crowd back into a whirlwind of frenzy after a planned lull in the M.C.'s sonic assault. Every gatherer rises to dance to the pulse of the techno-opera, and even Cynthia Dekoevend and Lord Abydon stand up to shake their bones. The two forget about decorum, finding themselves sublimated within the sound of pure delirium. For those who are not familiar with the experience, the joy of dancing to O Fortuna lies in the sensation that one gets where one feels as if he or she has physically joined with the source of all energy and motion in the universe. The overlapping chorus of voices in the song continuous to rise in power as the song progresses, and the force of its sound rolls across one's body like a natural disaster crossing a barren plain. Dancing to the sound creates the corporal illusion that the universe has decided to spin at ten times its usual rotation and forced the dancer to accompany it.

In the center of the maelstrom, the Nameless Blonde moves slowly. She has her eyes intently fixed upon a medium-built Jewish girl in a black turtleneck sweater and black jeans. The Jewish girl remains still, except for the motion of her hands, and these she lethargically runs across herself. They begin by her hips, move up to caress her own breasts, and then fleetingly stray around her neck into the short, dark helmet of her hair. The Nameless Blonde finds herself sliding her tongue lustfully across her lips. She continues to glance up and down the girl's lithe form.

In moments, the Nameless One becomes aware of his companion's distracted nature, and he wonders about the difference between her movements and the song's tempo. He glances at the Nameless Blonde in curiosity until she notices his stare and with a nod of her head points out the isolated brown-tanned waif gyrating fifteen feet

Before I can get my form to enact any motion, two comets, one red and one yellow, hurtle from the left and right sides of the skeletal head. They arch majestically in flight, their tails forming a bright path that stretches backwards into the void, and as they arrive closer to our position they slow dramatically to betray a multiplicity of dimensions within the aether. The two-dimensional aspect that I had come to believe in before the appearance of this ivory menace turns out to be an illusion, and I am able to see now that the void and the skull consist of various factors of space and time, and yet somehow more than those concepts. Eventually, the two celestial travelers settle into each of the skull's eye sockets. They flare up, burning like flaming retinas, and they illuminate the surrounding darkness. I gasp then, because I realize that the skull is no dead thing, but an actual living creature.

With my newfound vision, I find that the comets, themselves, are also alive and are spirits (or guardian angels as a mistaken group would say) from another realm. These spirits, along with the skull, comprise one complete entity, which then booms out across the expanse in a voice that frightens and surprises me. It intones, "and we shall feel you shiver, and we shall come, for we are the holy one." Strange colors flash through my head at this declaration. My external sight becomes enhanced, and I suddenly see endless lines of light crisscrossing through the void to form innumerable junctures, borders, and pathways. The spirit-flames within the skull seem to be the major focal points for these beams, and I begin to wonder what importance they have within this latticework of energy. Suddenly, I feel something shift inside of my form. The void shifts, also, and the spaces between the beams waver and unravel. A brilliant light from Beyond ripples and prods. My jaw drops open. I understand that I have been made aware of all the mystical doorways leading to another universe from this void. I have been given the gift of true sight and allowed to view that which has been hidden from common knowledge. As I continue to watch, the light moves and expands with living insistence. The brightness originates from an immortal being that exists in that hidden dimension, beyond the darkness, and in fact is that other universe. I realize now that the skull before me is nothing more than the face of that entity within this universe. After staring long and hard, I finally decipher the shape of the entity. It appears to my vision as a colossal flaming bird stretching across all creation. All motion and energy derive from it, and the beams of light act as extensions of its being. Where the extensions intersect mark the points of entry for that being into this universe. At that moment, I wake up laughing.

Intriguing is it not? I have my own interpretations as to what it means, but of course I will not share them with you until you have had the opportunity to dwell on the various images and contrive some interpretations of your own. One thing I should mention, though, is that shortly after awaking I stumbled across a large golden feather in my room. I have no recollection of obtaining this particular object, nor do I recall having noticed such an object prior to my reclining on my bed, yet, there it was pristine and enigmatic. Could I perhaps have been bestowed with my own Feather of Maat for having experienced such an epiphany? I hesitate to make an assumption one way or another.

Well, unfortunately, I must make an end to this missive. As always, I dreadfully detest this requisite closure, but I supposed I must do what I must do or else you will never receive this. It is just that in life there is no true ending, only doors leading to new rooms or pathways splitting off in various directions. Of course, there is one thing I can tell myself to pacify my mood. I know that this letter is not itself an actual ending. The threads of discussion contained within will be picked up by yourself, later, to be woven across the floor from them. She informs him that she had spoken to the girl earlier in the evening. She explains how she had convinced the girl to experiment with the Ecstasy floating about the place and how she had prepped the girl for an encounter later after deciding she was a luscious morsel. A wicked smile rips across the Nameless Blonde's face as she describes the subtle seduction of the mundane girl. Her excitable depiction causes the Nameless One to nod approvingly before flashing his own feral grin.

"A ménage a trios," he thinks. With a willing convert, this would prove a rather acceptable arrangement. The time to feed desire heats his blood, and without another thought he and the blonde slither over to the girl, winding through the other dancers like two snakes winding through grass.

The two Nocturnals surround the little Jewish girl with their bodies. They change their tempo in order to merge their body rhythms with hers, and when they accomplish this feat it appears to the surrounding attendees that the three figures are one convoluted pillar of flesh, a living sculpture to divine decadence. The sensual motions of the trio place the girl into an active trance, while her vision moves internal. She can no longer see the outer world with her eyes. Instead, she acts by touch, her entire universe becoming one with sensation, where the warm, frictional connection between herself and the two seducers engulfs her completely. With willing complaisance, the girl allows herself to be escorted off the dance floor and into a darkened corner. Her body slumps acceptingly against the wall as the Nameless Pair press against her, their lips seeking her neck.

Behind them, the Apotheosis song diminishes to a whisper, bringing a calmer atmosphere to the chamber in much the same way a snow fall in Winter quiets the mind of one who watches the large flakes float lazily to a shroud covered ground. The M.C. chooses to ease the gatherers toward the conclusion of tonight's festivities, and he shifts the music into an ambient textured sound. This week's gathering has served its purpose for the clan. The Nocturnals have been energized as much as their corporeal (and possibly spiritual) frames can handle, and they must now prepare to finish the night out in their own personal, and in many cases solitary manners. As is typically the case, the Divine Twins depart first, their egress mirroring their entrance with their arms about each other's waist and their hips rocking a cocky swagger. They pass close to Beltram, who leans against a wall with one leg braced perpendicular to it and reads over a pamphlet proclaiming an annual fetish party downtown. He debates making the trek up Broadway to attend and rationalizes that he should go if only to beat down the molten anger that Vernon has stirred in his breast. Across the chamber, Cynthia Dekoevend and Lord Abydon stroll stealthily toward the back exit. Cynthia publicly pretends to be having a fierce argument with Abydon and maintains a distance of six feet from him. Abydon asks what he has done to upset her, but she *into the threads of your own writing, and so on, creating a tapestry that shall never be finished. That is the real beauty of our correspondence and of existence—endless diversity and endless possibility. As the Bard once said, "life is but a stage, and we are but players". We live as part of an eternal story with a million protagonists, a million antagonists, and a million plots. We do not have the ability to create an ending for it.*

Shall I go on with this trite repetition of existential metaphors? No. You comprehend my point.

I apologize for blathering at you. You must understand, though, that this extensive speech is the diversion I use to escape the thoughts that plague me. The truth is I miss you dearly. My flesh longs for your touch, and this spatial distance between us proves abominable. These words are all I have to connect me to you in your absence.

There, I've said it. Now, enough of my maudlin behavior! I suppose I must finish this missive. . . and with the respect you deserve.

May your journeys in and out of Osiris' realm prove successful!

Phoenix

refuses to answer. His fear is palpable. Of course, he has done nothing. Cynthia simply prepares herself and him for the sadomasochistic games that she has planned for when they reach her haven. She wraps the bullwhip about her hand to clue him into her intentions, but he does not notice and continues to follow her like a doting pet. As for the posers in the group, Vernon and the German are nowhere to be seen. The left the gathering in frustration before O Fortuna began playing—Vernon for having been scolded like an aberrant child before the others and the German for not having been seen by anyone at all. Later, when the two hear of the intensity of the scene that erupted in the chamber during the apex of the Apotheosis song, they will rue the fact that they departed too soon. They will spend the upcoming week imagining the debauchery that ensued and will dream of experiencing it sometime. Finally, the rest of the gatherers file out of the chamber as silently as they entered. Few notice the Nameless One and Nameless Blonde have disappeared mysteriously. The duo's hungers have been partially sated, and they wish to pursue their further hungers away from the younger ones. Together, they race through the darkness that spawned them.

In the corner, the little Jewish girl sprawls limply on the floor. Her body stays immobile while she dreams of swimming through an ocean of flesh. Each rolling wave summons a miniature orgasm within her. These dreams will continue to lurk beneath her conscious mind until the next gathering. Then, she will feel this undeniable pull to return. She will seek out some fresh, young boy in a black turtleneck and Doc Martins. His nervous grin will summon her and will cause her to suffocate him with her forwardness on the dance floor. She will seduce him in the most direct manner possible, and she will return with him to her haven at the close of the ceremony. The sights she will show him will overwhelm his mundane mind, and in this way will she perpetuate the Nocturnal lifestyle, as others will continue to perpetuate it in various distilled forms down through the ages.

This is eternal life, forever and ever.

Made in the USA
Charleston, SC
17 August 2011